Hot Pink
in the City

a novel by

Medeia Sharif

Asma Bashir wants two things: a summer fling and her favorite '80s songs. During a trip to New York City to stay with relatives, she messes up in her pursuit of both. She loses track of the hunk she met on her airplane ride, and she does the most terrible thing she could possibly do to her strict uncle... ruin his most prized possession, a rare cassette tape.

A wild goose chase around Manhattan and Brooklyn to find a replacement tape yields many adventures—blackmail, theft, a chance to be a TV star, and so much more. Amid all this turmoil, Asma just might be able to find her crush in the busiest, most exciting city in the world.

Chapter One

People are being snatched right off the street. You'll be dragged into vans and alleyways.

Everyone is doing drugs, but not my children.

Don't go out alone. Always take someone with you, and never at night.

Waiting for this plane to take off, my parents' words stick in my head. News headlines run through my mind. But I'm not with my parents, and there's no TV in front of me. I'm on my own, and I have to entertain myself. My purse is in my lap with my smorgasbord of stuff. I take out my illicit makeup bag. Makeup isn't for me. I'm a tomboy and my parents don't allow me to wear it in public, yet I'm ready to be girly.

I pull out a compact and paint my face with blue and lavender eye shadow, hot pink cheeks, and fuchsia lips. Smiling, I like the shape of my colored lips. I pull at my sleeves so that both shoulders become bare, although I'm wearing a tank top underneath my shirt. For the last three years I've dressed like a boy, wearing shirts, shorts, and jeans. I'm the soccer star in the school and local papers for all the goals I make. My hair is always up with a scrunchie or banana clip, but I'm ready for a change. On this plane ride, I'll become a woman. I want to look like Kelly LeBrock, as if I stepped right out of a Pantene commercial. *Don't hate me because I'm beautiful.* With the way I'm dressed I'd shock my best friends, Misty and Tamara. They wouldn't believe it. Maybe I'll take a picture for them later.

I pull my scrunchie off so my straight hair tumbles down my shoulders. I have the clothes and makeup, but there's one more thing I need to be free, to be me, to be a woman. Where is it? I stick both hands inside the bowels of my purse to look.

"It's not here," I whisper. "Where is it?"

I don't care that I'm talking to myself and that people might look. The long fringes of my denim purse brush against my knees as I look for my Madonna mixtape. It has to be here. I only spent three hours making that tape, figuring out how to use my brother's new boom box with dual cassette players, with my mom yelling at me because she said the music was too loud. All that work for nothing when I can't listen to my favorite singer during this plane ride.

Our plane is filling up. I look up to see people shoving things in overhead compartments. I check out guys to distract my frazzled mind in hopes of quelling my panic over the missing tape. Blonds, brunets, green eyes, and hazel eyes walk past me. A screaming child hurts my ears.

But with the bad comes the good. After the child disappears to the back of the plane, a hunk with ripped muscles underneath a tight tank top, tawny skin the color of sweet caramel, and black hair with a braid across his shoulder reaches up to put his baggage away. Then he sits right next to me. I try not to stare, but it's hard when he's also checking me out.

"Hi," I say.

"Hello," he says.

His breath smells like peppermint, and his bulging arms remind me of ripe fruit that I want to take a bite of. Oh, and he looks like John Stamos. I never miss ABC's Friday night lineup because of him. As a soccer star, I get to ogle the boys' soccer team, the track team, the football team, and other boys at practice, admiring them from afar. My mom picks me up after practice or after a game, so it's not like I get a chance to talk to any of these boys, but here is one right in front of me.

"I'm Abe, short for Ibrahim," he says.

"I'm Asma," I say.

His name intrigues me. It sounds Middle Eastern. Other than relatives and family friends, I don't come by too many Middle Eastern people.

"I live in Miami, not too far from the airport," I say.

"I'm in North Miami."

We talk about what high schools we go to. He plays basketball and I play soccer. It's like a marriage of sports teams. The two of us had no knowledge of each other's existence in Miami, but we're headed to New York together. Maybe I can see him when I'm there, which will be hard since I'm going to visit family, and my uncle and aunt are as overprotective as my parents are.

"Excuse me, young man, but that's my seat," someone hovering over us says.

We both look up at a behemoth of a man, a John Candy look-alike who glowers down at us. "I'm 11-B," he says.

Abe lifts up his pelvis to reach the back pocket of his jeans—yes, I'm noticing his every move—and pulls out his boarding pass. "I'm sorry, I am in the wrong seat," he says. He gets up, pulling away from me, and retrieves his duffel bag. As he moves along with the tide of latecomers finding seats, he turns around to say something, but I can't hear him. I believe he said, "Talk to you later." I hope so.

An hour later, I use the restroom but don't see Abe on my way there, although some creepy guy can't keep his eyes off me. I scurry away from him. When I'm back in my seat, we hit some turbulence. My heartbeat quickens, but not just because of the shaking airplane. I'm traveling from Miami to New York to stay with my uncle and his family for two and a half weeks and I don't have any Madonna to listen to. "Who's

That Girl," "Like a Virgin," and "Dress You Up" play in my head, the tunes almost right in my mind since I know the lyrics by heart. Also they match the feelings I have for this boy I just met. But hearing the songs in my head isn't the same. I want to be able to stick a cassette in my Walkman and press Play. Her music makes me want to dance, see the world, and experience things. Inside of this cramped plane, my energy can't go anywhere.

Digging into my purse again, I find something to occupy my time: my scrapbook. I've kept it since sixth grade and I've put mementoes of all the important things that have happened to me inside it. There are letters from pen pals, pictures of me in local newspapers for high school soccer news, report cards, honor roll certificates, goofy pictures of my friends Tamara and Misty, and plenty of boys from my favorite shows and TV movies... and of course there's John Stamos.

With this summer in the greatest — and most dangerous — city in the world, I expect to add more to my scrapbook. I start now, though. There's glue and a stapler in my purse, because as a scrapbooker I have materials on hand. Taking my boarding pass, I glue it on a fresh sheet of paper. The book is thick, and wrinkly where I used too much glue. Still, this book is my life. I hope to fill it with many exciting things. My life has been plain, uneventful. I go to school and play soccer, day in and day out. A change is needed. This trip will give me one.

***

We land and people clap, which annoys me, because what did they think? That we would crash? I've been to New York before, but this time there's a difference. It's summer vacation, and my parents have sent me all by myself. They started doing that with my older brothers, sending them by themselves to visit relatives, which to them is safer than sending them to summer camp and cheaper than going all together as a family. My parents wanted to come to New York, but they need to save money for a new car. I begged them for a New York trip and my uncle wanted them to come, so my parents sent me to represent the family. Also, I'm old enough to travel by myself at sixteen. I will be the spokesperson for the Bashir family. It's so totally awesome that I'm on my own. I even feel closer to Madonna, since she lives in New York, not that it's likely I'll bump into her or anything.

My parents taught me to be afraid of the world. One wrong turn — being at the wrong place at the wrong time — can lead to death and destruction. Just standing by myself at the airport makes me nervous, which overrides the delicious freedom I have before me. I find my luggage and in the distance are the polar opposites, the creepy, oily guy who had been staring at me on the plane and Abe. The creepy guy looks like he's in a hurry, maybe to stalk a girl or something. I'm glad he's leaving. On the other hand, Abe is taking his time slinging his duffel bag across his shoulder and lifting another piece of luggage. I'm thrilled to see him. If I don't know where I'm at, I tend to follow others. Instead of reading the Exit signs, I follow Abe. His eyes don't catch mine, so he must not have any idea I'm behind him. His cute butt goes bump, bump, bump. Next to getting away with makeup and skimpy clothes — but not going overboard, because Uncle may complain and call my parents — maybe I can have a summer fling. I've never had one of those before. I've never experienced any sort of romance, period.

Abe is becoming more distant, and jeaned buttocks are blurring together. Too many people are wearing denim. I've lost him! "Asma!" someone yells. Does Abe remember my name? Of course, he must. It's only been a few hours since we've spoken before we took off.

"Asma!"

Oh, it's my uncle. Not Abe, the Uncle Jesse-John Stamos

look-alike, but my uncle-uncle. Uncle Farhad waves at me. His handlebar moustache looks ancient, seventies style when we're in the eighties. Even his polyester pants and plaid shirt look outdated. He needs to get with the times.

I walk to him, giving him a hug and kiss. His moustache tickles and abrades my cheek before he darts his hands behind me to get my luggage. So far, so good. He hasn't said anything about my altered appearance.

Uncle lifts my suitcase while I carry my duffel bag towards an Exit sign. Next thing, we're on a bus headed to Manhattan. I can't wait to call and write to Misty and Tamara. I told them I'd keep in touch with them during my stay here. They didn't seem thrilled that I was leaving, probably because they're going to miss me. Misty sort of dug into me before I left by saying, "New York isn't for a homebody like you." I know I don't go out much, unless it's for soccer games, but of course I'm not going to be a homebody during vacation.

I could stare out of the window forever, at all the New Yorkers and their dwellings... but my mind drifts to Madonna. I look through my purse again, but then it dawns on me that I changed purses last minute, picking a larger one, and I must not have emptied my other one out completely!

The mixtape has all my favorite songs. I don't have the money to purchase several brand new tapes. It'll be hard to glue myself to the radio to hear Madonna since Uncle is a despot when it comes to noise. He doesn't let my cousin, Nasreen, play the radio. She only plays it when he's gone. How am I going to live without Madonna? There's Cyndi Lauper, Lisa Lisa, Taylor Dayne, and some other favorites in my purse, but nothing beats Madonna. It's her sound, her chameleon hair and makeup, and the most rad costumes I've ever seen on anybody that beats out everyone else. I have no problem being me, but if I were to choose someone else's life I would want to be her. When I zone out in class I pretend I'm wearing a bustier and leggings.

"You look sad," Uncle says at a subway station, where we'll take a train for the rest of our journey.

I zip my purse closed and then fiddle with my neon bracelets. "I forgot to pack something," I say.

"Your aunt and I will provide," he says. "Don't worry about anything." His slight accent and deep voice are no comfort.

After numerous stops, which involves me studying people and the advertisements above my head, we're in the city of cities, the borough of boroughs. My worries over the lost tape and lost hunk vanish. The city calls to me and I'm answering. And whereas I live in the middle of nowhere in my Miami suburb, where I have to be driven or take a bus somewhere to do anything, New York has everything within reach. I'm sure I'll come across more than one record store. Then I can buy myself some Madonna. My parents gave me money for this trip; not enough for my liking, but they gave me some spending money. I won't waste anything on clothes or snacks. Madonna is worth a little bit of discomfort, and I shall have her music on this trip.

Chapter Two

Uncle lives in a basement apartment. We don't have basements or a subway system in Florida on account of the high water table—there's the stale joke my science teachers repeat about how if Florida were to be cut off from the rest of the states it would float away. I'm going to share a room with my cousin, Nasreen. She has a bunk bed, and since she's afraid of heights I always get the top bunk when I'm here. I get to watch people's torsos as they walk past the barred window.

A short flight of steps leads to a heavy metallic door. Inside I smell onions, garlic, and a whiff of walnuts. The first thing I see is a coat closet, and nailed to it is a framed collage of Egyptian singer Umm Kulthum. There are four pictures of her inside the frame. Uncle has several of these collage shrines around the apartment. I'm not the only one obsessed with a particular singer.

Everyone rushes to greet me with salaams. Cousin Nasreen is dressed in black, which is nothing new. She's into The Cure and channeling Robert Smith—I must look like Rainbow Brite next to her. Her eyeliner is heavy, which gives me hope that Uncle's home is a makeup-friendly place, so I can wear it for the next few weeks.

Nasreen's raccoon eyes brighten up, and she smothers me in a hug. Aunt Fatima's housedress flutters around her chubby legs. She greets me with kisses on both cheeks and a hug that squeezes the air out of me. Next is Cousin Omar. His dusky skin, large eyes, and long lashes face me. I want to hug him, even though I don't have the best history with him. The hug never happens. Instead of greeting me properly, the first thing that comes out of his mouth is, "What did you get me?"

If that were to happen in my house, he would receive a slap, but Uncle and Auntie are quite lax with him. "Don't be hasty," Uncle says in Farsi.

"Silly boy," Auntie chides.

Nasreen rolls her eyes.

"Baba, I want my presents."

I give Omar a nervous laugh, but I don't hand him his presents yet. Whenever I travel, my mother makes sure our suitcases are as heavy as bricks since she weighs them down with gifts for the family. I'm carrying jewelry, clothes, candies, and an assortment of things, but Omar can wait. He can play with his Atari or Transformers. Until I hand him his presents, he can bask in the glory of being the only boy in the family, which he's already been doing in his eight years of existence.

"Nasreen, take Asma to your room so she can rest after her flight," Auntie says.

I breathe a sigh of relief. I love my family and I'm grateful they're letting me stay here for a while, but being in this apartment is not much different from being at home. There are rules. Auntie is a housewife, like my mother. Uncle is unsmiling, same as my father. The only difference is my brothers are far more civilized than Omar. Behind the closed door of Nasreen's bedroom, I hear Omar run around, causing the floor to rumble. It's good that no one lives under them.

I leave my suitcase and duffel bag closed. Instead of unpacking right away, I jump to the top tier of the bunk bed. Omar used to sleep here, but he was complaining that Nasreen bothered him—yeah, right—and Auntie added a curtain to the family room alcove so he could have his own space. For all the tattling Omar does, one good thing came out of it. Nasreen has some privacy, with the exception of me being here now.

The room is so small that when I look down, I can see the top of Nasreen's inky black head as she sits at her desk, which looks like a card table with a tablecloth thrown on it. Piled on top of her desk are ripped-open envelopes. I see that the senders are all colleges and universities.

"Oh, you're shopping around for colleges since you'll be a senior soon," I say. That's totally responsible and ambitious of her. I have two more years to go, but have no clue what I'll be doing after high school. "Do you have your heart set on anyplace?"

Nasreen looks up, her eyes pitch-black in a pale face. She takes after Auntie, who's ghostly pale, while Omar and Uncle are tanned. Her stiff, hair-sprayed hair points up in spikes, as if multiple scissors are protruding from her head. "Like my parents are really going to let me go to the schools I want," she huffs.

"What do you mean?" I ask.

She shakes her head, her eyes brimming with tears. "I want to leave New York, go to Boston or Chicago or maybe even California, but Mom and Dad want me chained by their side. They want me to go to college here and live with them until I finish a degree program. But I want to travel and get out of this basement apartment."

"I like it here, but I can see how it's stifling."

"That's the right word for it. This is the only home I know, and it's like living in a sarcophagus. Dad doesn't even want to move because he's happy with how much he pays for rent, but we've been here since the seventies. In a few years, when it's 1990, I don't want to be here. I don't want to spend another decade in this apartment!"

"Aw, I'm sorry, Nasreen. I know how you feel. I don't want to live with my parents when I hit eighteen. I also want to see the world and do... things."

"They think I'll turn American and stuff. It's not like all Americans drink and do drugs. Anyway, we are in America. I wish they would get with the times."

My parents are the same. They're afraid I'll become too Amriki. They're always eyeballing my clothes, even the shorts and jeans I like to wear, and giving me the first degree about my friends and whereabouts. "I hope they see things your way."

"Well, I've talked until I'm blue in the face. I don't see them changing."

I don't see them changing their minds either, but I want to pep her up. "Maybe they will by the time you hit the end of your senior year."

Nasreen snorts. I don't blame her for being pessimistic. "I'm sorry for being such a downer," she says, her unshed tears clearing up. "Let's not talk about my problems. How was your trip?"

I tell her about the greasy guy, the huge walrus-like man who sat next to me, dreamy Abe who I barely got to know—I ramble on a few minutes about him—and then the Madonna mixtape that's missing. "I'm such a dingy to have forgotten it. I feel depressed that I don't have my favorite music with me!"

"I would feel lost if I didn't have my favorite songs with me."

"Don't rub it in."

"Hey, I know I'm not into Madonna like you, but I want to help you out. Let's make a new cassette with the blanks my father has. We just have to wait for Madonna songs to come on the radio and record them."

I'm sure that's a great idea. "What about your father?" I ask.

"He always hangs out with friends around this time of day," she says. "When the coast is clear, we'll use his radio. Mom doesn't mind. Dad is the one who doesn't like noise."

That sounds like a good plan. As I learned from my previous visits, Uncle is a noise Nazi. Unless it's his TV or radio playing, he accuses everyone else of being loud. "Turn it off right this minute!" he'll order. Nasreen uses his radio when he's out and then plays her tapes on her Walkman. Other than Uncle's music, Omar generates the only other tolerated noise. He can play his video games at a high volume and Uncle says nothing about it.

As Nasreen checks to see if the coast is clear, I unpack, placing my clothes in the two empty bottom drawers of Nasreen's dresser. My scrapbook goes under the two pillows of the top bed. I don't keep a diary, but in pictures and words the details of my life go in that book. What's great about a scrapbook is that because it's highly personal, with mainly images, only I can understand it. For example, there's a playbill from my school's performance of *The Mikado*, when my crush at the time, Keith, was performing. Instead of writing *I'm so in love with Keith Forsythe* in a diary, I have this playbill to remember him forever. My scrapbook is in a code only I understand.

I place the presents on top of a chair. I'll reluctantly give Omar packages of Matchbox cars and Gobots later. He has enough toys as is. Uncle and Omar have plastered their playthings over the entire living room. This apartment is definitely an all-boys terrain. This tiny bedroom is Nasreen's space and Auntie has the kitchen, while everything else revolves around the guys. Even my house is more liberal, because my mom has the family room to herself and I have a spacious bedroom. This will be my longest stay in New York. I'm sure I'll be out most of the time. I hope the cramped quarters of this basement won't make me stir-crazy.

After unpacking and placing my empty bag and case under the bunk bed, I sigh. When I turn around to see if I left anything on the floor or bed, I see the door is ajar and a lone brown eye is looking at me. I almost shriek. Pesky Omar, snooping to look at his presents. I hear the thump of his feet as he runs off. I clutch my heart and calm down. He's only a harmless, bratty little boy.

***

Uncle is gone. It's Sunday, and he spends weekend afternoons with friends at the McDonalds two blocks away. He used to take Nasreen and me with him years ago in between sightseeing. He and his friends—mainly Iranians—occupy a booth, talking for an hour or so about politics and finances, subjects that don't interest me in the least bit. My Farsi is a bit rusty since over the years I've been talking English to my parents, but I understood Uncle and his friends when he took me to hang out with them. Now that we're older and don't need babysitting, he no longer takes us, thank goodness. I used to be bored out of my mind.

Auntie is in the kitchen making something delicious. She pays us no mind as Nasreen and I explore the living room. Uncle sure has many electronics. He used to keep them in the family room before it was converted to Omar's room. Behind closed curtains we hear the brat playing a game. It sounds like *Mario Brothers*—the jumping sound effect confirms it. I wish I could play it, since I have the games at home, but Omar is territorial, same as his father.

Uncle has his own games since he's the gadget man. One side of the living room has shelves and an entertainment system devoted to his musical pleasures. He has bootleg cassettes from Turkey, Iran, Lebanon... every Middle Eastern country is represented. There's Vigen Derderian, Shohreh Solati, Ibrahim Tatlises, and Umm Kulthum. There are names I recognize, since some of these tapes are the same ones my family has, and others are new to me. The cassettes have white inserts with the names of the singers and bands scribbled on the side, or poorly made inserts with cheesy graphics and photos of the singers.

What we're after is sitting by itself adjacent to the TV: a

shortwave radio with a cassette player. Uncle likes to listen to news straight from the Middle East. When Nasreen turns the radio on, we hear someone speak Arabic in a staticky voice. Nasreen turns the dial until we're hearing the BBC.

"Cool," I say. My parents also have a shortwave radio, but they barely use it. Uncle, on the other hand, plays his several times a day. He's very much into keeping abreast of news from the homeland. There's a stack of newspapers printed in Farsi and Arabic on the coffee table.

I look through his boxes of cassettes, gravitating to the ones that have an actual insert. I see mustachioed men and gorgeous women heavily made up. To the right of me, I'm eye to eye with Umm Kulthum. Uncle has a second collage of her in the living room next to his entertainment center; there are four pictures, two color and two black and white, of her in various stages of life, from her youth all the way to the seventies before her death. There's a third collage in the master bedroom. Uncle sure loves her. He's had these framed collages since I could remember. I pull my eyes away from her image so I can focus on my own music idol.

"Okay, let's find a blank tape," Nasreen says. "I don't want my cousin to stay here without anything to listen to."

I look through a different box and pull out several blank tapes. I just need one since we only have an hour or two until Uncle comes home, but I have a vision that I'll record each one of Madonna's songs, and she has many songs. The woman is a prolific goddess. Each album is an entity onto itself as her style of music and fashion changes. She's like ten women rolled into one.

Nasreen flips the switch to FM and pulls the antennae up. We tune into a station that plays freestyle. I bop my head and shimmy my shoulders to the dance music of Exposé, but Nasreen changes to a rock station. Her body sways to rancid guitar music, which sounds like a symphony of saws to me.

"Hurry up and find Madonna before your father comes

home," I urge.

We sit on the carpeted floor, getting comfortable, but then a sound coming from behind us chills me. It's worse than Freddy Krueger or that freaky doll in *Child's Play*. Those are movies, but the little monster behind me is real and can cause some serious damage since he's everyone's favorite little guy.

"What are you two doing?" Omar asks.

I turn around to face his wicked little grin. One side of his mouth is turned up higher than the other in a truly diabolical way. I look askance at Nasreen, and her throat goes up and down in a nervous gulp. He's small, yet he can do a lot of damage. There's no shaking him. He's like a bloodhound on a trail, snooping on me not too long ago and now in my face. In the past, I was here with family, and I didn't have too many encounters with him since he was younger and less outspoken. It dawns on me that I'm going to spend a prolonged period with this unsavory little boy.

"We're not... not doing anything," I stammer.

"Let's make our cousin feel at home," Nasreen says.

Omar's face widens, blowing up. He's like a balloon, full of devious notions and the itch to snitch. "You're not supposed to be playing with Baba's radio!"

"Lower your voice," Nasreen orders between clenched teeth, being big sisterly and menacing.

"Relax," I say.

"You're ruining Asma's stay here!"

"Please, give us a moment alone," I plead.

Omar's face shrinks, the redness leaving his cheeks. I believe our pleading has calmed him down. He opens his mouth, surely to apologize or tell us to proceed with what we're doing. After all, I am family. He is a cold little booger, but I refuse to believe he's heartless.

"I'm telling Baba!" he yells. "You two will be in so much trouble. Oooh, I'm telling..."

Chapter Three

"Nasreen, taste this rice!" Auntie commands. She walks out of the kitchen with a spoon in hand, her short, curly hair rising in all directions from the humidity of the kitchen. "Blow on it," she says.

Nasreen looks from her brother to her mother. I'm also waiting to see if Omar will say anything. His eyes stay on us, as if his mother isn't interrupting. He wears his smirk with pride.

My cousin crosses her eyes as the wooden spoon, with a huge dollop of rice at the end of it, nears her. She blows on it and then takes a bite. Auntie pulls the spoon up so every grain ends up in Nasreen's mouth. Her eyes are fixated on her daughter, as if the fate of the world is resting on Nasreen's shoulders.

A beginning of a smile plays on her lips. "How is it for softness?" Auntie asks.

"It's fine, Mom," Nasreen says.

Her lips turn up some more. "And for salt?"

"It's just right."

Auntie fully smiles, unleashing her happiness on us. She has received validation for her cooking. She walks back to the kitchen, her bubble butt causing her dress to rock like a pendulum.

With Auntie out of the way, Omar goes back to

grinning. "You know that Baba doesn't want you using his radio."

"There are exceptions," Nasreen says. "For example, we have a guest in the house."

"Baba has never mentioned these exceptions."

"Come on, it's just for an hour," I say.

"I never use his radio, because I have something called respect. Maybe you two need to learn about it. What if you break his radio? He'll be so mad. And even if you don't break it, he still won't like the idea that you're using it while he's out. I know your game, Nasreen. I see how you turn the dial and switches to the way he left them. I've been nice enough not to mention what you've been doing all year."

"You're such a tattletale, I swear," Nasreen says.

Auntie walks in again, spoon in hand. She has a serious look on her face. She needs more praise. Her presence relieves me, because her son acts less obnoxious around her. Auntie and Uncle think he's an angel; they would never believe how evil he really is.

"How is this gravy?" she asks in her accented English. "Blow on it."

Nasreen rolls her eyes, but she does as asked. Auntie crouches down so Nasreen can blow on the spoon and its thick, red contents, and then in her mouth it goes. Auntie smiles, waiting for the compliment. Her eyebrows go up and down, willing the accolades to erupt. Everyone tells Auntie she's a good cook, but she fishes for compliments so she can hear it again and again.

"It's delicious, Mom," Nasreen says.

"Did I make it too spicy?"

"No."

"I added some lemon juice. Is it too acidic?"

"No."

"Should I add onion?"

"Why not?"

"Yes, I should." Auntie leaves, but I'd like her to stay. Omar behaves, kind of, when she's around. When the sound of onions being chopped begins, Omar rubs his hands together and smirks.

Devious demon child! He knows he can dangle this threat over Nasreen's head any time he wants. During my last vacation, I witnessed Nasreen breaking out her pocket money to pay for his silence. Nasreen had an unlit cigarette in her purse, given to her by a friend. She did admit to me that she planned on smoking it since she's never tried cigarettes, but she never got a chance to. Omar said he spilled her purse's contents by accident and found it, which is bull. He probably was snooping, which he's good at. Omar took the cigarette and then blackmailed her. He has a cigar box full of money that goes inside the locked coat closet by the front door. The little booger saves his allowance and blackmail money. But I don't want Nasreen to lose money for what she's doing now, since she's trying to help me find Madonna music. This is my fault, so I'll have to fix this problem.

"I ran out of money, and I don't want to be the only one of my friends who can't buy anything at the candy store after we finish playing ball," he says.

Nasreen's hand disappears inside her pants pocket, but I grab it by the wrist. "I have something for you," I say. "And it's better than candy."

"What do you have?" Omar asks, curiosity softening the evil glee on his face.

"Let me show you..." I get up, beckon him to Nasreen's room, and hand him his presents, which I wanted to give to him tonight—I have to get rid of him now, though. He's the barrier between Madonna and me. Omar jumps up and down—he seems to do that a lot—and he even puts his arm around my waist, which is the closest thing to a hug I'll get from him. Not that I want a hug from him. I want him out of my way.

***

I sit back down with Nasreen. Omar is behind his curtain. I hear the metallic click of Gobots and the crashing of toy cars. Now we can get down to business.

Nasreen tunes the dial. The sweet sounds of FM fill the apartment. She finds a pop station, Z100. Commercials are playing, so we wait. The first one is an advertisement for a Madonna concert at Madison Square Garden. I heard about it in the news, but now that I'm in New York maybe by some miracle I can go.

"Do you think Uncle will let us see Madonna?" I ask.

"My dad isn't one to let me go to concerts. I begged him to see U2 awhile back, and he wouldn't let me go."

"But I'm a guest." Middle Eastern people are quite hospitable to guests. My own parents drop whatever they're doing to cater to them, whether it's serving them food or picking them up from the airport. There is an issue of money, since I'm sure tickets for Madonna are pricey. I hope I can figure something out.

I grab one of the blank tapes I had pulled off a shelf. Nasreen takes it from me and inspects it. On both sides of the tape are slender strips of bright white stickers that are blank. I'll find a pen and label it when we're done. She pops the cassette in.

Commercials are over and I hear the beginning of "Who's That Girl."

"Now!" I command.

Nasreen hits the Play and Record buttons simultaneously. She also cranks the volume all the way up so we can get a high quality recording. The sound drowns out Auntie's kitchen noises and Omar's racket.

I place my head on Nasreen's shoulder as Madonna's voice bathes me in a warm glow. I want to dance—next to soccer it's my other favorite activity—but in this small living room I'm afraid to knock something down and ruin the recording. The song is about to end. With other singers I don't pay attention to the endings of their songs, and I even fast forward to the next song, but I listen to Madonna's songs to the very end.

"Nasreen, taste this meat and tell me how it is!" Auntie orders.

"Nooo!" I screech. My heart jumps into my throat. The recorder must have caught Auntie's voice.

Auntie walks out of the kitchen just when the song ends. She was joyful a moment ago, but now she's frowning, as if she's performing surgery. Cooking is serious business for her, as music is for me. I'm upset, because I was so close to having a perfect recording of that song. Maybe if I play back the tape it won't sound that bad... but on top of Auntie's voice is my protestation of her interruption.

My aunt doesn't acknowledge my anger and surprise. Madonna's voice must have drowned out my outrage. Nasreen is her focus. Her daughter is her official taste tester. Maybe my cousin can make it into those Pepsi versus Coke commercials, make a name for herself in the cola wars. I stop the cassette and lower the volume as Auntie bends down, aiming a fork into Nasreen's mouth. Madonna transitions into Duran Duran. I usually picture myself marrying John Taylor when I hear them, but I can't fantasize with Auntie in front of me. She's ruined any chances of daydreaming.

"How is it?" Auntie wants to know, hovering over us like the chef of the gods. She won't pull her eyes off her daughter, who can bless or condemn with her judgment.

"Hmmm," Nasreen mumbles, still chewing.

"Is it too dry?" she intones.

"No, it's moist."

"How is it for salt?"

"Fine."

Auntie breaks out into a smile, her eyes squinting shut. Meanwhile, I'm seething inside. "I'm so glad you like it."

"Is that all?" Nasreen wonders, voicing my thought, because I'm too polite to ask.

"I'll see... I'm off to finish this." She walks away, and I'm hoping she's not coming back.

"I think that's it with her," Nasreen says. "Unless she wants me to taste the salad."

"Please, no." I shake my head. My aunt has always been like this, having people test and praise her food, but today her timing is wrong.

"Let's see how this sounds." Nasreen presses Rewind. Now that we're no longer recording and I'm not afraid of moving around, I put my arms in the air and gyrate my hips, grinding my butt into the living room carpet as Madonna croons one of my favorites. I'm still sitting down, close to the radio, because this recording seems fragile. I'm positive it's bad.

Then I hear it. *Nasreen, taste this meat and tell me how it is*, followed by me protesting, *Noooooo!* The recorder caught everything. The last thirty seconds of the song are good for nothing. We'll have to play the radio forever, while Uncle is out, until we find this song again and other Madonna hits. I can even call radio stations with my requests to speed up the process. At least Uncle is going to work tomorrow. He writes Farsi and Arabic subtitles for a movie company, and he freelances as a translator for books. With him gone tomorrow, we'll have more time to look for songs.

The last three seconds of the song wind down in volume, and I hear Auntie's first question regarding the sliced cut of beef. Then I hear something else.

There's no more Madonna, Nasreen, or Auntie. This blank tape has something else after "Who's That Girl." Poetic wailing and Arabic song follows.

"What's this?" Nasreen asks.

"I don't know," I say. "We didn't record this."

The voice trills on, coming from the soulful gut of

whoever is singing. Nasreen and I lift our heads to look each other in the eye. She grabs the cassette holder and studies the label. The front is blank, with lined paper for note-taking. Then she turns it so we can look at the spine.

My jaw drops.

Most of the cassettes in the boxes have labels on the spine as well as in the front, but this only had writing on the spine and on the inner flap of the insert. *Umm Kulthum*, it says in English on the spine. On the inner flap is a list of songs in Arabic.

The breath is knocked out of me. "We recorded over one of Uncle's tapes!" I gasp. "He'll kill us."

"Holy moly shit," Nasreen says. "We did. I thought this was blank."

"I did too."

"Dad sometimes has duplicates. Let's see if he has other Umm Kulthum tapes. She's his favorite singer!"

"I know!"

There are three shallow boxes, and we look through all of them. Let there be another Umm Kulthum tape with the same songs. Pretty please with a cherry on top. Umm Kulthum, who's deceased, has to be the most popular Middle Eastern singer out there. She was Egyptian, but people all over the world adore her, and my uncle is one of her biggest fans. Not only does he have all these collages, but he's also gone to her live concerts before he immigrated here.

I don't want to fall into my Uncle's bad graces on my first day in town. What if he treats me like his own child and grounds me? Maybe he'll lock his radio up when he's not here so that I have no access to Madonna. I can forget asking him for permission to see her in concert. My parents will get wind of this and never trust me again to travel by myself. I'll be a prisoner during my stay in New York as well as in Miami when I go back home to a tongue-lashing. *You shamed the family!* I hear my mother's voice in my head. Yes, I did something bad. How do I make things right?

Chapter Four

You must respect your aunt and uncle, follow all their rules, and be careful with their home and belongings. Don't make a mess. Pick up after yourself and offer to do chores.

Do not make yourself and the family look bad!

My parents' words fill up my head. They're all the way in Florida, but I can hear them loud and clear.

I'm practically useless when it comes to deciphering Arabic and Farsi script, since I recognize random letters and sounds, but Nasreen is better at reading it than me. We split ourselves between boxes. I check out one box of cassettes, she the other. For the third one, we lay everything out on the floor and inspect together. I hope Uncle doesn't notice that everything is out of order. I don't think he alphabetized his collection, but I'm sure he'll notice the cassettes aren't in the order he last left them.

"Okay, here's some more Umm," Nasreen says. She finds a cassette with a picture of the singer. Her hair is in a bouffant and she's wearing sunglasses. She looks majestic in a beautiful ball gown.

"Open it," I say.

We look inside. Actually, it's other artists singing covers to her songs based on Nasreen's reading of Farsi. "This isn't her," she says.

I look at the tape we recorded over and the spool looks intact. The tape has no scars or other marks on it. It looks practically new. What did we do?

We search some more. We find another cassette that's a mixtape of several Arabic singers, but according to what Uncle scrawled on the insert there's only one Umm song on it.

"So the cassette we ruined was the best and only Kulthum tape Uncle had?" I ask.

"Apparently so," Nasreen says. Her voice is flat. Even the spikes of her hair look like they're drooping. No amount of hairspray can uplift us. We made a boo-boo of massive proportions.

Omar is behind the curtain, still playing with his new gifts and enjoying the toys I handed him. At least he doesn't know about this. "My dad only has a soft drink and fries at McDonalds since he's really there for his friends," Nasreen says. "Mom is almost done with dinner, so he should be here soonish."

I gasp at the thought of him coming home. I also think about tonight, which is when I should be calling my parents to tell them I arrived here safe and sound. I told them I would call around nine. I can't tell them about what I did. They'll be so embarrassed. This will totally be the last trip they ever send me on. I hope my parents don't take soccer away from me, because I live for practices and games—that sport is in my blood. They've taken away phone and TV privileges in the past, so I wouldn't be surprised if they limit my freedom even more.

"We have to hide the evidence," I say.

Nasreen grabs the Madonna-Aunt's voice-my protest-Umm Kulthum tape, and we rush into her room. I wish her door had a lock, but I'm pretty sure I gave Omar enough goodies to occupy him until late tonight.

"So what should we do?" Nasreen asks.

"Well, we definitely can't have Uncle or anyone else find the tape," I say. "Once he hears Madonna and my voice, he'll know I did this and that you're my accomplice. We need to destroy this tape but keep the box and insert for when we find a replacement."

"Good idea. Some of those cassettes were gifts, but my dad does buy tapes here. I'm sure we'll find a replacement."

We brainstorm and do the following: Nasreen finds a Bon Jovi cassette box minus the tape since she lent it to a friend who never returned it, and I take a black marker and scribble all over the ruined tape so that if anyone were to find it he or she would never figure it was Uncle's cassette. Then Nasreen cuts the spool of the tape with scissors. I slip the ruined tape into the Bon Jovi holder. The Bon Jovi-destroyed Umm cassette is now in my purse so I can dispose of it in an outdoor garbage can the next time I go out. Nasreen puts the original cassette box under a stack of clothes in her closet for the replacement tape we'll find. We act like we're in Iran, with intelligence officers spying on us. Stories of the old country told to us by our parents have seeped into our bones. We're really going out of our way to disguise, hide, and throw out the cassette we bungled.

"It's not like your dad is the secret police," I say.

Nasreen snorts. "You don't live with him," she says. "They open my mail. Colleges send me material I requested, and sometimes I don't see it until weeks later. Don't underestimate my parents."

That sucks. Even my parents respect my privacy by not opening my mail. I guess we are doing the right thing by getting rid of this tape. Poor Umm. She had a brilliant singing voice, and I messed with it. Umm is like Madonna to Uncle. I covered my room with Madonna posters, and his home has Umm collages. Umm has a magical voice that transports you somewhere else—I'm positive if I knew Arabic then this feeling would be stronger for me—and Madonna takes me someplace else, into her world where everything is cool. Hours ago I was upset that I forgot to pack Madonna with me, and Uncle will feel the same way when he can't find this tape.

I vow to find a tape to replace it since I ruined Uncle's best copy of her songs. If only the write-protect tabs had been broken in, then we never would have recorded over it. It's amazing how something so small, a tiny piece of plastic, makes a world of difference.

"Ooooooh, I'm telling," someone murmurs behind the door.

I jump, and so does Nasreen. We look behind us and see a big brown eye peering at us through a crack in the door. Sneaky little booger.

"You two are up to no good," Omar says, opening the door wider.

"You little..." Nasreen utters.

"Watch it," he says, sounding far older than his age. "You can't afford to say anything bad about me. Why did one of you say 'replacement' awhile ago? Did you mess up one of Baba's tapes? You know he loves his music, and he never wanted either one of you touching his tapes or his radio."

What I would do if he were my brother, but I can't do anything. I'm in his home. I swallow a lump in my throat. All the balls are in his corner. I already thought I paid for his affections and his silence not too long ago, but I didn't give him enough. He wants more. But what more can we give him?

"So which tape did you break?" he asks. "And how? Did it snap in two while you were playing it? Did you record over it? What happened? What singer was it?"

He lists all the possibilities of what can happen to a fragile tape, but we're not telling him anything. "Don't worry about it," I say.

"I'm not going to be quiet about this. What can the two of you do for me? Huh? And make it snappy, because I have a busy evening ahead of me."

Chapter Five

Nasreen and I sit in her room eating *lokum*, aka Turkish delight. It's this gelatinous, sweet thing covered with powder with nuts inside. The powder falls onto my lap and it's even funnier on Nasreen, who's dressed in black. She looks upset, although the powder across her mouth, chin, and shirt look comical. Sitting on the floor of her room, we have to cheer ourselves up somehow. Auntie doesn't have chocolate on hand in the kitchen, but there's lokum.

A chair stands in front of the door so Omar can't snoop on us any longer. He's the reason we're glum and eating sugar. He demanded twenty dollars, so both of us are ten dollars poorer. He didn't even know all the details of our crime, but the looks on our faces and our hiding in Nasreen's room tipped him off that we did something bad.

I might end up completely poor by the time I leave if Omar consistently blackmails us. He promised to stay silent about the broken tape with this twenty-dollar fee, but I don't trust him. He'll always have this thing to hold over our heads. And if I keep losing money, I'll definitely never ever get Madonna tickets. There's no use asking Uncle if I can even go if I don't have the money, and it would raise my parents' suspicions if I were to ask them for more money. If they stick some bills in an envelope, I'll get it in a few days, but I can't ask. Mom and Dad thought they had given me adequate funds for this trip. And some trip it is. I just got here and I'm already miserable. The excitement of the city and the possibilities within it disappear. Omar's smug face, my lighter wallet, and the Kulthum tape I destroyed swim in my head.

Not only is a tin can of lokum by us, but we also have Uncle's radio. No longer wanting to be in the living room, a stone's throw from Omar's curtained alcove, we took the radio so we can use it in the privacy of Nasreen's room. I have a blank tape—an actual blank tape this time—sitting on Nasreen's dresser, but I'm not in the mood to do any recording. Listening to Madonna would put me in a better mood, but I don't have the will to find her music. Also, with Auntie around, I don't know if she'll barge in and ruin things—we barricaded the door, so she might pound on it with one fist while a spoonful of food is in the other. Not only do we need Uncle out of the way, but we need Auntie out of the apartment too, although it seems like she never leaves.

I hear the clash of pots and pans as she finishes making dinner. "We need to put all this stuff away," Nasreen mumbles. "My dad is a creature of habit, and, looking at the clock, he should be here any minute."

Instead of being afraid that he's coming, that he'll find us with his radio in the bedroom instead of in the living room, where there's a dent in the carpet from its bulk sitting there constantly, I'm slow to move. I lift the radio, move the chair aside, and walk into the living room. The dent is dark against light beige. I put the radio back on the carpet, between the sofa and entertainment system, and it fits inside the dent perfectly. I'm laying this radio to rest. It brought us to no good this afternoon.

The phone rings, and Auntie rushes to it, as if she's going to miss something important. She doesn't want anyone to wait, as if that makes her a bad person. It isn't wrong to let people wait instead of catering to them all the time. All she does is try to make others happy. I wonder what makes her happy, or maybe what she's already doing is all she wants.

When she picks up the phone and begins to speak Farsi, it's apparent she's talking to a friend. Her eyes roll up to the ceiling in ecstasy, and she's smiling. Auntie is friendly, a hostess, a people person, a face stuffer who wants you to eat everything on the plate — after all, there are people starving in Ethiopia, and we should be grateful for what we have.

"Yes, our niece is here... Farhad's niece, from his mother's side... she's sixteen... I haven't really thought about marriage, but it does sound like a good idea... your nephew Nabil sounds like a good match for her."

The lokum sits heavy in my stomach. It seems like all the older women in my family are looking for husbands for me. At home my mother talks about boys she knows, young men her friends have told her about, sons of friends. Meanwhile, I don't want to be tied down. I'm still in school! And I'd like to find someone on my own. Ideas of the summer fling I've daydreamed about float in my head, but the people around me want to set me up with someone right now or in the near future.

Auntie hangs up the phone. "Don't look like that," she smiles. "My friend saw a picture of you and thinks you're quite pretty for her nephew. But we're not putting pressure on you."

Yeah, right. It sounds like pressure to me.

"Dinner's almost ready and your uncle is almost home, so why don't you wash up. It looks like you've eaten lokum. I'm so glad you like it. Oh, before you eat dinner, maybe you should call your parents already and let them know you're okay instead of waiting until tonight. You might go to bed early and miss calling them."

I wash my hands and return to the living room. I look at the green curtains that mask the alcove. My monster of a little cousin is behind them. He'll probably hear my entire conversation with my parents. He's in a central location where he can watch everyone. Outside of his room, he's sneaking around, opening doors, and peeking in at people. Nasty little spy.

I pick up the phone and call my mother. "How are you, Asma?" she asks. She talks in a hybrid of Farsi and English, switching between the two. "How was your flight?"

"Great." I don't tell her about wearing makeup, handsome Abe, and I most certainly don't breathe a word about the Kulthum tape.

"You be on your best behavior. We trust you by yourself over there. We shouldn't hear a negative word from your uncle and aunt, but I know we won't hear such things."

"Right." I gulp. This is too much for me. I ruined a tape containing music from the Madonna of the Middle East, I lost money to my bratty cousin, and my aunt is mentioning the word "marriage" and me in her conversations to friends. I have many more days of this...

***

Nasreen's taste-testing and Auntie interrupting my music recording at least had one good result. Dinner is fantastic. Succulent beef, a rich gravy, and delicate rice fill up my tummy, although I'm not eating as much as I normally do. My nerves rattle through me. I quake hearing the clattering of forks, knives, and saltshakers. Nasreen picks at her food. Omar quickly finishes dinner and asks if he can leave. With these long summer days, he can play outside in the evenings with his friends. Just as Omar is about to leave, there's a knock on the door. I see a glimpse of four of his friends, some taller and older-looking than him, and Omar goes with them to a playground across the street. Before the door closes on him and his friends, I stare at his back pockets, picturing my money in them. If he knew what was going on inside of me, he probably would have stayed to torture me. My eyes dart up to my uncle and aunt. Nasreen is also watching. We're particularly interested in Uncle. Auntie doesn't touch the music collection because it's her husband's evening-time hobby.

After dinner, Uncle makes tea. Auntie does practically everything around the home, but he'll actually make tea. It's his one domestic chore. He puts a kettle on the stove, and then he organizes newspapers and magazines on the coffee table. I sit at the small dining table that's between the kitchen and living room. The tea is done. Uncle asks if I want any and I say no. I'm too busy observing him that I don't want to have anything scorch my throat.

I notice some faint cracks in the wall and the grains of rice that have fallen on the tablecloth. I'm a daydreamer, someone who can count ceiling tiles in class or study the inside of her mouth with her tongue when taking a test not studied for. Now my mind isn't able to distract itself. Uncle blows on his tea and sips on it. Sluuuuurp. Sluuuuurp. Sluuuuurp. I've never heard that sound come from a human before, but that's Uncle's loud tea-drinking sound. He sounds like a vacuum suction.

He eats a piece of baklava. Auntie's baklava has the right amount of buttery crispiness in each layer. Since I had lokum with pistachio already, I pass on the baklava with walnuts. Maybe tomorrow I'll taste it, if there's even a tomorrow. It's amazing how a small tape seems to be dictating my life, my happiness, and my whole entire stay in a city I was looking forward to exploring. It doesn't even matter that I'm in New York City. I could be in London, Paris, or Amsterdam... my actions from earlier today would dim the brightness of any city.

It's as I predicted. Uncle heads to his shelf, where all the cassettes are. "What am I in the mood for?" he says in English.

"Why don't you play something instrumental?" Nasreen asks. "Don't you love it when you get a break from a singer's voice?"

"I do like that, but I want to hear lyrics, something that will put me in a good mood. How about Googoosh?"

"Yes, play Googoosh!" Nasreen insists. She's a bit loud and fake. She doesn't even like that type of music. If it's not in English and doesn't involve guitars, she doesn't care to hear it.

Uncle's thin, brown fingers skim through his cassettes and records. They have large, bubbly Arabic, Farsi, or some other foreign script, while the bootleg materials have inserts covered in marker. If only the markings on the Kulthum tape had been more conspicuous—I would have noticed that a full tape was in the cassette player and we wouldn't have recorded over it. This dread wouldn't be seizing me right now.

"I love Googoosh, but I will play her some other time. I think I'll play Umm Kulthum."

My body becomes rigid while Nasreen turns pale—I mean, paler than normal.

"Where is that tape?" Uncle mumbles.

"I know, play some Fereydoun Farrokhzad!" Nasreen squeaks.

"No, no, I want to hear Umm Kulthum," Uncle protests. "All day long I've thought about listening to 'Ya Zalemni,' my favorite song of hers." The shelf of cassettes, records, and 8-track cassettes is Uncle's world, his old world, him bringing his country to this new one. I was born here and have never been in the Middle East, but when I listen to my parents' songs, images of mountains, rivers, hills, deserts, men in turbans, and women in headscarves come to mind. That music conjures up an exotic place that's part of me, a place I don't completely know about. I'm sure the music must mean even more to Uncle since he grew up there. And I ruined a slice of the old country because I was dying to have Madonna songs. It's up to me to fix this, to distract him so he drops this idea of hearing Umm.

"Where is that tape?" he asks. "I cannot find it!"

"I have my camera with me," I say. "Why don't we take

some pictures? My parents asked me to take pictures of all of you, and I don't want to leave it for the last minute."

"Yes, it's picture time," Auntie gushes with a smile. "Go get your camera."

That was close, and I'm glad I caught my aunt's attention. Her enthusiasm spreads to Uncle. I get my camera from my purse and bring it. The problem is that Uncle and Auntie believe in being stiff in pictures. Uncle wants to take a picture of Nasreen and me, and he tells us to sit with our hands in our laps. Since when do I sit like that? Auntie lifts my hair so that some of it hits my shoulders. She licks her finger and takes a swipe of Nasreen's eye shadow that has smeared under her eyes. When she gets out of our way, Uncle snaps a picture of us like that.

This is so uncomfortable, but this is how they take pictures here. Nasreen has shown me family albums before, and it's like looking through pages and pages of mummies. Everyone is standing straight, arms at their sides, or sitting down with their hands in their laps. Everyone faces forward, with no profiles or semiprofiles to be seen. I love it when I'm with my friends and we take pictures, because I jump up, stick my tongue out, and put my arms around people, and my face can be seen at all types of angles. Uncle and Auntie are against lively pictures for some reason.

"Now Nasreen will take a picture of Asma and us," Auntie says.

I stand by the window, against the radiator, and Uncle and Auntie sandwich me. They have their arms at their sides as if they're in the military. I make a move to put my arms around them. "No, no," Auntie says. "Stay still and look at the camera."

I put my arms down, feeling awkward and unnatural. These pictures are going to look horrible. We take turns snapping pictures so that I get to sit or stand—like a mummy—with all my relatives, except Omar who's still out.

Auntie made me promise to leave some film for him. With my camera back in its bag, I sit down. I sigh in relief, from both having the picture-taking ordeal out of the way and from Uncle being distracted from his request to hear Umm. I was wrong about that, though.

He's back to the shelves looking for the tape. "I could have sworn I put the tape in this box."

What more can I do? We just spent a half hour taking pictures, with Auntie and Uncle fussing over me on how to pose. I have to do something else.

"Owww!" I howl, grabbing my head with both hands. My fingers clutch sticky tendrils of hair covered in Aqua Net. "Owwwwwwww!"

"What's wrong?" Uncle asks.

"What's going on?" Auntie asks.

"I think I have a migraine," I say. I cradle my head in both hands, my eyes squeezed shut. "It hurts so much."

"Get some aspirin," Uncle orders Auntie.

"That'll help, but I need some peace and quiet," I say, lowering my voice, because it pains me to hear any type of loud sound. I'm pretending and hating myself for doing so, but I'll do anything to get Uncle's mind off Umm Kulthum.

"Lie down," Auntie says. She grabs me by the arm and leads me to Nasreen's bedroom as if I'm an invalid. She pushes me by the small of my back up the bunk bed. I close my eyes, but then open them when Auntie hands me a glass of water and aspirin. Sitting up, I swipe my hand over my mouth and drink the water. The aspirin is tightly stuck in the folds of my palm. I'll save it for when I have a real headache.

Lights are turned off, voices are hushed, and everyone is quiet because of me. "No, no, don't go in there right now," Auntie tells Nasreen. "Go there when you're ready to sleep. And you don't play any music to disturb your niece." I'd love to talk to Nasreen right now, but Auntie is keeping her away from me because of my faux illness. I'll talk to her when I'm feeling better in a few hours. I'd also like to brush my teeth and wash the thick makeup off my face. I can't pretend I'm ill every single night whenever Uncle mentions he has a yen to hear Umm. I need to find a replacement tape, and fast.

Chapter Six

I wake up in the middle of the night in a sweat with a loud voice pounding into my head. My heart jumps in my throat, and then I remember where I am. I'm in Uncle's basement apartment, which I used to think was cool, but now I perceive it as freakish and deathly. Disoriented, I sit up, high above the floor since I'm on the top level of the bunk bed, yet I'm looking straight through a window, where the curtains have opened, probably from the movements of my tossing and turning. Between the exterior bars of the window and the iron fence that's a barrier between the stairway and the street, I see people's headless bodies float by. A woman talks into a payphone, which is right outside the window. Payphone users have disturbed my sleep during previous visits.

"I have no money for a taxi!" the woman screams.

I'm not the only one with money problems, I see.

Memories of what I've done hit me hard. The tape. Omar's greedy hands reaching out for money. My mom thinking everything's okay when clearly I messed up on arrival. What am I going to do?

I scoot closer to the window and part the curtains some more. It's past midnight, but people are still out, walking, alone or with others, in sneakers, in pumps, in sandals. Someone walks by with a boom box blaring, the large eyes of the speaker meeting my own eyes. Angling my head to look down the street, I see lights of restaurants and bars that are still open. It's hard finding places in Miami that are open this late, but in New York anything's possible. That's what I need to believe: the possibilities that lie in this city and how anything can be fixed. I'm in a big city, not my hokey little suburb in Miami. Somewhere in Manhattan there has to be another Umm Kulthum tape I can purchase to replace the one I destroyed.

A huge moth the size of a cockroach lands on the window, and I have to stifle a scream. Insects scare the crap out of me. I pull the curtains together and lie back down, feeling a little bit better. I dip my head underneath my upper tier to check on Nasreen. She's curled up in a ball. I'm about to lie back down, but then her eyes fly wide open, the whites bright and illuminated by a nightlight. I jump, gripping the sides of my mattress. "What are you doing up?" I ask.

"What are you doing up, young lady?" she counters.

"I can't sleep."

"Neither can I. So what shall we do about this sleeplessness?"

"I don't know." I shrug. "Can we watch TV?"

"Not unless you want the Wizard of Oz snitching to my parents," Nasreen whispers.

I chuckle, but not too loud. Uncle is the noise Nazi, and Omar hides behind his curtain like a fascist tyrant. Even though he's in the alcove, I wouldn't be surprised if he's up at this time to watch us.

"If you want to watch TV, it has to be my way," she says.

"What way is that?" I ask.

"Come to my lair..."

I climb down, intrigued. I didn't know Nasreen had a lair. The apartment isn't that big, so I wonder where she'll take me to watch TV. Omar dominates the living room, since he has his curtained nook there, and the kitchen and dining area are too close to the master bedroom, where Auntie and Uncle are.

Expecting Nasreen to take me somewhere, she instead opens her closet. It's a large closet or maybe a small walk-in. She invites me into the darkness. Inside, she pulls a lightbulb chain that illuminates us and puts a towel at the bottom of the door. "We can't have any light escape," she says.

Whoa, she's really against having Uncle find out what she does. What parents don't understand is that their children have secret selves, secret lives. My parents would never believe what I paste in my scrapbook, the thoughts in my head, my dreams of being a famous singer and dancer, and the boys who woo me in my daydreams. Now Nasreen is showing me another side to her, but I'm still confused. "Why are we here?" I ask.

"Sit down," she says. She sits on the floor, and I follow suit, crossing my legs. I notice the walls, which have crayon drawings all over them. Looking at the doodles Nasreen did as a child, I feel like I'm studying prehistoric man. She drew the sun and moon, and people with circles, triangles, and squares for heads.

"I didn't know you were an artist," I say.

"Trust me that I received punishment for my artwork as a kid," she says. "My parents were horrified that I did this in my closet. I even drew on the living room and kitchen walls."

I smile, thinking about a rebellious little Nasreen. I position my limbs the best I can. I'm feeling cramped with our bodies hitting the wall and door. Nasreen already pushed hangers to the side, but her clothes still brush the back of my head. The light overhead is dim, and, as my eyes adjust, Nasreen takes a pile of clothes and throws them aside to reveal a small, six-inch TV. "One of our neighbors left this outside the garbage chute, and one day after school I rescued it. Dad doesn't know I have it. This is how I watch TV late at night, but I keep the sound low so no one can hear it."

One cousin lives behind a curtain and another in a closet. Interesting. And it's kind of scary how Uncle is so controlling. Even my parents don't complain if I stay up late to watch TV or listen to my Walkman. They admonish me that I should go to bed early so I can wake early, but they don't make a big deal if I go to sleep at one or two in the morning. As I inhale the scent of stale perfume and mothballs, taking in this odd room within a room that Nasreen hides in, she turns the black-and-white TV on, adjusts the rabbit ears, and tunes in to a syndicated sitcom. *Three's Company* segues into *Too Close for Comfort*. Those shows are all the same to me with their canned laughter and repeated storylines, but I actually laugh, but not too loud. We can't get loud at all.

"I haven't told any of my friends I watch TV or read in this closet," Nasreen whispers, her pajama bottoms rubbing against mine. "You better not breathe a word."

"Of course not. And who'd believe me?" We're in a different level in this basement apartment, and I'm touched Nasreen has shown me her sanctum.

During the commercials, Nasreen shares more about her desire to leave the basement, New York, bratty Omar, and her overprotective parents. She's played drums in her high school band class, but her father won't allow her to have a drum set at home. She itches to join a band, read her poems at a poetry café, go on a road trip... the more I listen to her, the more I want to do some of these things and help her live her dreams.

"Nasreen, I hope you get to do all of this," I whisper. "I also want more in life. I want to be on TV, dance, sing, do things I've barely had practice in since my parents won't let me take formal lessons. I only know how to do some of these things playing around with friends. I want to be seen."

"We both want recognition."

I squeeze her arm and put my head on her shoulder. Despite the anxiety of destroying Uncle's tape, I'm glad to spend this closeted time with my cousin. We continue watching TV, but the shows become less entertaining as it turns to early morning. "*Josie and the Pussycats* comes on in an hour," she says. "That's about all that's good at this time."

"That's the only cartoon I still watch. I love that show. And I also love *Jem*."

"Band babes all the way."

"Do you have the Yellow Pages?" I ask.

"Why?" she says.

"I want to see if there are any Middle Eastern shops in the area while we wait for *Josie* to come on."

"I'll be right back," she says. Getting out of the closet is a big deal. She turns the TV off, pulls the towel away from the door, and shoves clothes and hangers out of her way. I'm alone for two minutes, taking in the true silence of the apartment, minus the people outside the windows and the restless city. I now see why this closet is a haven for Nasreen.

"Here you go," she says when she comes back. She puts the towel in its place, sits down, and turns the TV back on.

I grab the phone book and look through the sections for markets, grocery stores, and specialty stores. I find a few ads and listings for Middle Eastern stores. "Be careful," Nasreen says. "This is my dad's main phonebook. The other ones are old."

Sheesh, everything is about not upsetting her dad. Meanwhile, we did the worst thing we could yesterday... which is why I have this heavy book in my lap in the first place. I'm going to correct this mistake. "Let's go to these stores today while your dad is at work," I say, pointing at some listings.

Nasreen peruses the pages. "Okay, I know where most of these are," she says. "I've been in one or two. We'll get to know the subway system like never before."

"Anything, as long as I don't have another night like last night. First doing something stupid and then doing whatever it took to hide it. I can't have a headache every day I'm here."

Time flies as we look at the small print of the pages. We can't write in the book, so Nasreen jots down addresses on a notepad. When we look up, *Josie and the Pussycats* is playing.

"Let's go to sleep after this," Nasreen drawls.

"I can barely keep my eyes open." I yawn.

We watch the show, yawning every few minutes, unaware of the time. Nasreen seems more engaged in watching TV, while I'm getting tired of it. On the notepad I draft letters to Tamara and Misty. I don't want to write to them about my Umm problem, because I can imagine them rolling their eyes. *Asma is in the greatest city in the world, and she messed up. She can't even enjoy her stay. We should've gone instead of her.* Why do they sound so catty in my head when they're my friends? When I'm talking to them they have a way of being sarcastic, with playful putdowns, but that's how friends are.

"What are you writing?" Nasreen asks.

"Letters to my friends back home."

"Okay. I wish you could call them, but my dad gets ballistic about long-distance phone bills."

My parents are also sensitive about those calls. They do their best to call at certain times when the rates go down. I've heard my parents yell into the phone after eleven at night, reaching far-flung relatives at that time for the best rates. I brought a pencil case full of coins with me, because I do plan on calling my friends on a payphone. Even though the one outside the apartment generates a lot of noise outside the bedroom window, I'll be using it to call Misty and Tamara.

When we emerge out of the closet, we blink at the wall clock. It'll be dawn soon. That was the best few hours I've ever spent in a closet, outside of trying on outfits. "We must do this again," I say.

"Okay, but next time we should bring some snacks,"

Nasreen says.

"Yeah, maybe popcorn."

"No, nothing that pops."

I giggle. Nasreen puts the phonebook and her notepad on her desk, and we're back in bed. My eyes droop and open in time to people's footsteps. Through a part in the curtains I'm still watching people pass by, fewer than there were hours ago, but they're still out there. At this time of morning there isn't a soul out on the streets in my suburb, but this city is always alive. This city will provide an Umm Kulthum tape to save Nasreen and me from Uncle's wrath and my parents' distrust.

Chapter Seven

    I have this wonderful dream. David Copperfield walks into the basement apartment with that beautiful bush of hair on top of his head, brooding eyes, and hands that gesticulate and are ready to perform some magic. He levitates through the apartment, stops in the middle of the living room, and stares into my eyes. We're alone, as we should be. He'll be my hero. He waves his hands in the air, and an Umm Kulthum tape falls into my hands. I am saved.

    My lids flutter open. I don't want the image of the tape to disappear. I really want to believe David is nearby performing magic. The man walked through the Great Wall of China, floated across the Grand Canyon, and made the Statue of Liberty disappear. Surely he can help me with my problem.

    Waking up at ten in the morning, I realize David is just a dream. He can join John Stamos and Patrick Swayze in my stable of imaginary boyfriends.

    I'm groggy after a late night with Nasreen. That was a much different experience than my last time in a closet with someone. Months ago I went to a party, after begging and convincing my parents it was an innocent birthday celebration, and I ended up kissing a guy in a closet. It was Brad, a boy from math class. He has dirty-blond hair and a cute face, but his braces were a turnoff. That five-second kiss, with boys timing us outside and girls giggling, felt like forever as I worried about swallowing any food stuck in his braces. He had been eating Doritos minutes before. Maybe I can have a real kiss this summer. Again, I ponder the idea of a fling. The Uncle Jesse look-alike, Abe, runs through my mind. If I weren't so obsessed now with replacing the Umm tape, I'd be checking out guys... and not just in my head. My libido isn't the same with this worrying.

So my closet time with Nasreen was unusual, but it made me feel closer to her. I used to feel a bit formal around her, but now I know I'm more than a relative. We're friends. With no hesitation I shake her awake. "We have to get busy today," I tell her.

She opens her eyes to slits and then puts an arm up to shield herself from sunlight. She looks different without the heavy, raccoon eye makeup. She's much prettier, the same way Ally Sheedy was better-looking after her makeover in *The Breakfast Club*.

"Okay, I'll get ready."

We need to hit the streets today and visit stores to get a replacement tape. I imagine once we get this tape, we'll never have to worry about Uncle searching for Kulthum and coming up empty-handed, and we won't have to admit to what we had done.

An hour later we're showered and dressed. Auntie straightens my collar and fixes my sleeves, skirting around my shoulders. She avoids touching people's shoulders, because both shoulders carry angels, one writing down your good deeds and the other the bad deeds. I'm hoping my good deeds outweigh the bad, but that might not be the case with the way my summer is going.

Before we leave, Auntie blows air on us, as if she's a rotating fan head. Not only does she do it to Nasreen, but she also grabs me, puckers up, and blows air around my face. She whispers prayers in Arabic between breaths.

"It's for protection," Nasreen says when we're outside.

"I'm sorry my mom blew on you."

"No, that's sweet of her." Strange, but sweet. My mom never does that.

We take the subway to the first store. My eyes don't waver from the windows as I look for station signs to see what the next stop is. Nasreen looks bored, but I can imagine that people take for granted what's right under their nose. In stations and on the streets I throw change into hats as people sing, play violins, and dance. People-watching is so much fun in New York.

On 14th Street, one store we visit doesn't have the tape we want, but we buy some lokum, getting white powder all over ourselves as we eat it under the awning of the store. In a Canal Street store we rummage through the small selection of cassettes, but we don't find Umm. On the covers we see heavily made-up women in elaborate dresses, both modern and traditional, but they all look like recent releases.

"Come on, let's go," Nasreen says impatiently whenever I check out the fares of street vendors. The street-shopping is amazing, even better than store items because of the prices. After we buy hot dogs and sit on the rim of a fountain to eat lunch, I put on a pair of earrings I just bought, feeling the rhinestone drops graze my shoulders. I know I shouldn't be spending what little money I have, but I should enjoy Manhattan right now, since Uncle may soon banish me from his home. From a park entrance I watch vendors wind toys with kids eagerly looking on. Businessmen, tourists, beautiful boys, and gorgeous girls walk past me. I love this city.

We travel uptown again, and the fourth store in Manhattan has nothing for us. We see plenty of newspapers, magazines, and some music... but not Umm. Most of these stores are for groceries when we need to look through a full music selection. "Let's try this place in Brooklyn that we wrote down," Nasreen says, wiping the sweat off her brow.

Brooklyn sounds like a long trip, but we have to do

whatever it takes to replace that tape. We're back on the subway. The subway has taken me underground and above ground, I've seen darkness and light, we've stood on many platforms, we've been through regular waist-high turnstiles and then the full-body ones, we've walked through tunnels, gone up and down steps, we've switched lines... I now feel like a subway-traveling pro, but the journey isn't over.

Brooklyn seems like an entirely different city. The skyline is shorter and streets are more residential. After walking ten minutes from the subway station, we're at the last store on our list. The street is quiet, and all of a sudden there's a loud burst of voices to the right of us. There's a school across the street that children exit from.

"What's that about?" I ask.

"Summer school letting out," Nasreen says. "My own school has similar hours. Thankfully I passed all my classes and don't need anything this summer."

I observe little kids rush towards parents and older middle-school kids walk off alone. "I hope this is it," I say, turning my attention back to the store.

"Me too, or we're screwed," Nasreen says.

The window displays cassettes and videos, with signs about various imports. This looks like the most promising place, so a small light ignites in me. I follow Nasreen inside to see a wonderful sight — there are rows of cassettes, videos, and records. There are no groceries, no newspapers, and no clothes. This is strictly an entertainment stop.

"Hello!" a round man with a bushy moustache greets us with a lilting accent. His stomach juts out of his body as if he were pregnant, and he has protuberant moles on his face. "Welcome to my store. How may I help you young ladies?"

Behind him is another man sitting next to a burgundy curtain. It's reminiscent of Omar's curtain, which reminds me of what's waiting for us back home. The man looks like a relative of the greeter, with the same round look and moles.

His thinning hair is greasy, wrapped around his scalp in a comb-over. I don't like the way he's looking at us, especially at me. His eyes linger up and down my body. I eyeball him back and then look away from him. The nerve of that guy.

"We're looking for Umm Kulthum tapes," Nasreen says, getting to the point.

"Do you have any?" I ask.

"Umm Kulthum? I love her! She's very popular."

"Yes, she is," I say. "So you have her cassettes?"

"Let me see what I have..."

While he's searching, I look around. Even though the relative-looking guy is creeping me out, I near the curtain because I'm wondering if there's a selection behind there as well.

"No, do not walk through," the stranger rasps, his voice harsher than the other man's. He continues to study me from the top of my head to my sneakered feet.

"Sorry," I say. It must be a backroom or office of some kind. I walk back to Nasreen. We stand, watching the first man search for Umm.

The store is small, with narrow aisles, and I imagine his large belly must occasionally knock things off shelves. He proves me wrong, because he's quite graceful and knows where everything is. "I have three records... but you said tapes... ah, here's a tape." He pulls it out from underneath the register. It's a bootleg, and when he pulls out the cassette from the holder it even has a Sony label on it—the tape we destroyed was Sony. I swing my purse closer to my chest, because I'm ready to buy it. The tape has to be mine. Even if it doesn't match the one we destroyed song for song, it's better than nothing.

"It's all her greatest hits," he says, ever the salesman.

"We'll take it," I say.

"How much?" Nasreen says. Her purse is across her body, like mine is, which is how she told me we need to wear it in the city—not the way I normally sling it on my shoulder as if I'm at the mall. The city is dangerous. Normally I feel comfortable around relatives and other Middle Eastern people, because those people are like me, from the same fabric so to speak, but these men unsettle me. The relative guy stares at me harder, and the greeter gives off a bad vibe. His smile widens until gold fillings wink at us from the back of his mouth.

"Err, what's the price?" I ask.

"This tape is very special," he says. "Also this tape isn't on the shelves. It's from my personal collection. It's not an official recording."

"We know," Nasreen prods. "We don't have a problem with a bootleg. What's the price?"

"The cost is one..."

One dollar? My heart soars. This is like hitting up flea markets back in Miami and finding great dollar deals. The rhinestone earrings on my ears and the turquoise scarf I'm using as a belt were both a dollar. I never knock a dollar deal.

"One dollar," Nasreen murmurs. I hear the thrum of joy underneath her words. I grab her hand and she reciprocates with a squeeze. Replacing the tape is easier than we thought.

"Not one dollar, young lady. The tape costs one hundred dollars."

Chapter Eight

Dizziness hits me. I've been in the hot sun and I've only had a soda to drink since leaving the basement apartment. Something else adds to the surreal spinning feeling that wraps around my head. I believe the man in front of me asked for an exorbitant amount of money, which I don't have. There must be some mistake.

"What!" I screech.

"A hundred dollars?" Nasreen asks. "Is the cassette gold-plated or something?"

"It's the only one I have," the man says. "And it's straight from an Egyptian bazaar. It's a bit old, made when cassettes were gaining popularity. It's practically an antique. I bought this myself, and it carries many memories from my time in Cairo. Also, again, it's not an official tape. It's not on the shelves, and it's not really on sale. I pulled it out because you expressed an interest."

This is highway robbery. Where are we going to get that type of money? Between Omar ripping me off and basic living expenses during my trip, I don't have that amount of money to spare. I can definitely forget about getting Madonna tickets too. One... hundred... dollars. For a tape.

"Listen, what are your names?" he asks.

"Why?" Nasreen asks, narrowing her eyes, far more street smart than I am, because I was about to blurt my name.

"I can take down your number, and if I get some more Kulthum tapes, I'll sell you a newer one for much less. But I can't part with this one that easily."

"Can't you just copy the tape?" I ask. "You must have the equipment since this is a music and video store." Many of Uncle's tapes are bootleg, and this is a bootleg as well. One copy can't hurt, right?

"Ahh, I don't really do that," the man says. "It is against my way. I don't want to dilute the quality. I've tried that before, and the quality really is affected. Also, I've only played this a few times because I don't want to wear it out."

Nasreen snorts. "So we can't have a bootleg of a bootleg."

"No, sorry," the man says, ever smiling, ever happy he's ruined our day. We find what we want, but this man has his reasons on why it's overpriced and we can't have it.

"This isn't fair!" I say.

"Life isn't fair." He shrugs. Now he's sounding like a parent or a teacher. I want to get out of here, even though he's holding exactly what we need. I'm beat after spending hours looking for this tape. It looks like a glass of water on a sizzling day, but I can't have a sip of it.

Nasreen asks for a pen and paper. I see she's writing down fake names. She calls herself Shireen and I'm Isma. That's easy to remember, not that it's likely I'll see this guy again... although he has the answer to our problem. The Middle Eastern community seems small. I wouldn't be surprised if Uncle or someone else I know has been to this store before. Fake names are a good idea. Nasreen also writes down a phone number, which makes me feel ill at ease.

"This is the number to the payphone outside my window," Nasreen whispers to me. "No way am I giving out our house number."

"This guy is a total rip-off," I whisper back.

"Yeah, tell me about it."

"Good-bye," I say aloud.

"I'm Wahib, by the way," the owner says, "and over there is my brother Tahir. This is our store."

Tahir winks at us. Nasreen's body shakes. Wahib hands us two business cards with the address and phone of the store next to a colorful picture of a cassette tape. I don't see myself calling him, but maybe I can put this in my scrapbook.

"Okay, bye," Nasreen says. She grabs my hand and pulls me out of here, away from the money-hungry storeowner and his perverted brother. I can breathe freely again. The air is humid and there's no breeze, but I gulp it in. I need some water soon. I envy the boys a block away who are jumping through the spray of a fire hydrant.

We've smeared the notepad paper full of addresses from handling it all day. We look out across the street at the school. There are a few kids lingering out front, but then they dissipate. It's time for us to go home too.

"Maybe I can tell my dad I ran out of funds and he can send me some money," I say. "I don't know if that'll work since he said he gave me enough. I guess he thought his nice little daughter isn't capable of getting into a situation like this."

"We can look harder and find another tape," Nasreen says. "There's no way this is the only Kulthum tape in the whole city."

"But we went to all those places today," I say. "This was it."

Nasreen's lips are a grim slash. Her lined eyes look tired. "You're right," she says. "Let's just go home, and maybe tomorrow we can resolve this. Hey, maybe we can explore the other boroughs, even other states. Maybe there's something to be found in New Jersey."

I don't feel good about all the traveling we may have to do, which might not be fruitful. What if we go to other stores and they don't produce a tape? Also, I enjoyed the city somewhat today, but the tape is pressing on my mind and the time we took going to all the stores were draining. "Great. I hope Uncle doesn't have a sudden hankering for Kulthum tonight," I say.

"Yeah, we can only distract my dad for so long," Nasreen says.

***

There's one more hour to go until Uncle's home. I'm watching a music show when Madonna comes on. I have the urge to take Uncle's stereo and pull it to the TV to capture the sound, which I've done in my own home, but I can't do that. Auntie is walking in and out of the living room, and Omar is playing with his toys behind his curtain. I miss the privacy of my bedroom back home. I suppose I could've bought a Madonna tape while I was out today, but the Middle Eastern stores didn't have them. Also, I have to be money conscious. I'll buy Madonna after I get the Kulthum problem out of the way.

Auntie continues with her superstitions. She blew on me hours ago, and now she's frowning at me because my bedroom slippers are flipped over on the floor. Using her foot, she nudges them right side up. "That's bad luck," she says.

My dad said that once, that it's bad luck if shoes are lying upside down. I don't know how much worse my luck can get. When Auntie leaves the living room, I put the slippers back on my feet.

I continue to sit by myself in the living room, watching TV. Nasreen is in her room looking through college and scholarship applications. She's deep in that paperwork and I don't want to disturb her. Anyway, this is a great time to figure out how to make some money fast. Maybe I can get a brief summer job, although that would totally ruin my vacation. Why would I travel somewhere to work? Any job I'd be hired for would be some grueling, horrible job like waiting tables or operating a cash register — not my idea of fun.

I look at the gold bracelets on my wrist. Maybe I can pawn them, but they're family heirlooms. They're twenty-one karat, thick bangles given to me by my mother, given to her by her mother, and they wouldn't let me live if I got rid of them. Money... I need some right now. I'm good at dancing and playing soccer. I also write a mean essay—I always get As in English, and if it weren't for soccer I'd have joined the journalism or yearbook staff. I have talents, so there must be something I can do for some quick bucks in a short amount of time.

Auntie walks out of the kitchen, a spoon in her hand. She's seeking her daughter out for her taste-testing abilities. Her eyes skim over me, and then she goes into Nasreen's room. "Habibti, taste this for me. What are you doing?"

"What does it look like I'm doing?" Nasreen asks.

"Why are you applying to a college in Los Angeles? No, no, I won't have this. You cannot go there."

"If I get a scholarship and a job to support myself, I'll go wherever I please!"

"How dare you yell at your mother..."

They're arguing in a mix of Farsi and English, their voices muffled behind the wall, yet I can hear everything since the door is open. This doesn't look good.

"I don't want to stay with you, Mom. Get over it. I want to leave this apartment. I want to leave New York."

"Why do you want to leave us? Have we not provided for you? Don't we love you?"

"You don't get it."

But I do. I know that intense yearning for freedom. I've felt it many times myself. I've felt it at school, when I'm out by myself, at the airport, in the airplane... being out on my own, no parents telling me what to do, making my own decisions, the freedom to make mistakes I can learn from. Why is that so much to ask for?

I hear a sniffle. I'm not sure whether it's Nasreen or her

mother who's begun crying. They lower their voices, repeating their argument. Auntie walks out of the room, rice still on her spoon. She's frowning, walking past me and ignoring me. Nasreen rebelled by refusing to eat the offering, which I've never seen her do before. I want to rush in and comfort her, but I'll give her privacy. It's bad enough she shares her room with me during my stay and that she just had a tiff with her mother. When I'm in a crying mood, I don't want anyone talking to me.

I wonder if there's anything I can do to help, but things aren't right with me either. How am I able to help someone else when I can't help myself? My first priority is to replace the tape, but I also want to help my cousin. It'll be tough since Uncle and Auntie think the way they do, but there must be some way to crack their old-fashioned resolve.

With this heavy stuff swirling in my head, I decide it's time to call my friends in Florida. I sneak into Nasreen's room to get a handful of quarters from underneath the clothes in my drawer as well as the letters I wrote to my friends last night. She bends her head down and doesn't look at me. Auntie is also in a funky mood, chopping up vegetables and not saying anything when I tell her, "I'm going to drop off these letters in a mailbox."

First I go around the corner to a heavily graffitied mailbox, and then I return to the building to where the payphone is. I deposit a coin and after I dial Tamara's number, an operator asks me for more money. Ugh, long distance is a pain in the ass.

Tamara's mom answers and then puts her on the phone. "Hey," I say. "I wanted to check up on you."

"Hey, girly," she says. "I miss you. How's New York?"

"It's great."

"Doing anything wild?"

"Well, I met this guy, but I lost sight of him at the airport."

"Oh, Asma, you should've been more aggressive, be more of a go-getter."

"I know," I admit.

Please deposit twenty-five cents, an automated message rudely interrupts.

"Can you hear me?" I ask.

"Yeah, I can now," Tamara says. "Get me a souvenir, at least a keychain."

"Err, okay. Hey, something else happened, something sort of bad —"

"Bad? To a goody-goody like you?"

"Yes, it's because I left a Madonna tape at home."

"You and Madonna! It's not that big a deal."

"But there's more..."

Please deposit twenty-five cents.

I give the greedy payphone more money while picturing myself throttling whoever owns that voice. *Stop stealing my money!* I want to scream. I also want to tell Tamara to stop interrupting so I can tell her about my problem with the Umm tape.

"Hey, I have to go," Tamara says.

"But I didn't tell you about what happened to me last night."

"Oh, Asma, I really gotta go. Write it in a letter. My toenails are dry and I gotta get to my fingernails now..."

She makes a kissy sound on the phone before the line goes dead — I'm not sure if I ran out of money or if she hung up on me. It's as if I were caught with my pants down around my ankles. I wanted to tell her something important, to get something off my chest, but I couldn't. I also didn't write about my problem in my letter because I'm paranoid about Uncle. What if he saw the letters lying around and decided to read them, the same way he reads Nasreen's mail?

I'll call Tamara in a few days and maybe then we'll have a normal conversation. I also owe Misty a call, although

I'm not eager to talk to her. I love my friends, but there are things about them that irk me. They seem too busy to listen to me, and they're full of putdowns they insist are nothing more than playful teasing—*Because we love you*, they say. And Tamara thinks I'm a goody-goody. New York is pulling me out of that goody-goody shell, bringing out a side of me I didn't know existed.

Chapter Nine

I've never liked newspapers. I only look through them when teachers ask me to do a current events assignment, but now I'm looking through a stack of them. I bought several newspapers to look through the ads sections. Nasreen is helping me. We're looking for moneymaking opportunities. I'm glad to be with her. Compared to my friends, she listens, is nonjudgmental, and seems supportive of me. Maybe it's because we're in a bind, but I've always enjoyed her company, and this summer we're becoming closer.

Her regular black-and-white TV — not the one hidden in the closet, since she never takes that one out from her hiding place — is playing in the background as we sit on the floor together. Since she's peering down at the newspaper, her eyes look like two black holes in her face. I myself am wearing frosted blue-and-purple eye shadow and a pink shirt and shorts. I'm all about color and positivity. Maybe she needs to add some bright colors to her wardrobe to spruce up her outlook and future.

"Have you found anything?" she asks.

"Not really," I reply.

I found a few summer jobs for nannies, but I can't disappear for days to take care of anyone's kids. I also found waitressing and cashier jobs. Maybe I can call them and see if it's during the daytime. Uncle won't miss me during the day since he's at work, but if it's nighttime I can forget it. I eye the business exec and medical jobs. Dollar signs swim in my head, but of course I'm not qualified for those positions.

It's early in the afternoon, so soaps are playing. I glance up and down to look at *The Young and the Restless*. The opening theme of piano and violins sounds depressing to me now, when that usually signals an hour of mindless, yet entertaining, melodrama. I'm not dying to know what's going on with Victor, Nikki, and the Abbots. I need money.

After circling a few ads that catch my attention, I put the paper down and give my eyes a rest. I'm tired of reading the tiny print. It hasn't even been an hour, but it feels like it's been much longer. Commercials come on, and I switch the channel, but every channel is playing them. I stop switching when a radio DJ tells me I need to listen to his evening show for a chance to win Madonna tickets. Wouldn't that be cool? If only I were able to listen to the radio in the evening, but I can't since Uncle is here and he listens to the radio at that time. Then another commercial comes on. There's a new entertainment show in town called *NYC Dance Off*, and they're looking for people to audition to make it onto their dance floor. I wonder how long that show is. Maybe I can do that.

"Nasreen, what do you think about that show?" I ask.

Her eyes are on the TV since she's also taking a break. "No way, Asma. You can't go on those shows. You're not a *Solid Gold* dancer or one of those girls on *Soul Train* shaking her rump."

"But I dance really well."

"You won't be staying too long and can't commit to something like that."

"This looks like a one-time thing. It said you show up to sing and dance for an audition and then dance for at least three of their shows. That's something I can do. I love to dance. Everyone says I'm good at it."

"Uh-uh." Nasreen shakes her head. She's so negative.

How can anyone have such a dour outlook on life? I can't blame her too much. She wants one thing, to leave New York, and she's not getting that. If I can find a way to help her, I'll do whatever it takes during my stay. Maybe I can have a talk with Uncle and Auntie, even though they never seem to side with her. Everything is about Omar. He gets everything he wants while they push Nasreen to the side. If I can show Nasreen it's possible to make dreams come true, she'll be more open to my own dreams. And I have many dreams. I think about Madonna. Then I daydream about being on the stage myself, singing and dancing. There's no way I'll ever be like Madonna, since she's one of a kind, but I imagine I have Taylor Dayne's voice, Stacey Q's hair, and Janet Jackson's moves.

"You want to try recording something else?" Nasreen says, pushing the newspapers to the side.

"Sure. But what if your mother walks in on us again?"

"The living room isn't an ideal spot with Mom and Omar close by. Let's try to record something here."

"I don't know if I want to move your Uncle's stereo into this room again."

"Yeah, he might notice it shifted out of its spot, and then we can't have Omar see we've unplugged it. Maybe we can record something from the TV."

Nasreen opens her closet and pulls out a dirty beige tape recorder, the kind without a radio that's strictly for cassette playing. "There's a show that comes on around this time, *NYC Dance Off*, the one you were just mentioning," she says, switching channels until we see dancers gyrating. Seeing them makes me want to move.

I untangle the cord of the tape recorder, which Nasreen plugs in. She takes a blank cassette and puts it in. "Hold on, we better try it first," I say, remembering the tape we destroyed.

"You're right."

We play a few minutes of the tape, fast forward it, and press Play again. Yeah, it's blank.

"Next up is Madonna's 'True Blue,'" the pretty host with big shoulder pads and bigger hair says. "Let's go to the dance floor to see people groove to this hit..."

"Hurry up, let's press Record," I squeal.

Nasreen holds the recorder up to the TV, raises the volume, and just as the song comes on I hit the Record and Play buttons. This is quite awkward. Nasreen mouths "okay" to let me know her arms aren't tired. I've done this before at home, putting a stereo up to the TV to catch a song I like. The recorder has to be close to the TV and the volume has to be really high to get a good recording.

"Habibti!" someone outside the door says.

"Noooo!" I shriek.

"Habibiti, come taste this for me. Why is the TV so loud? I hope I'm not interrupting anything. Nasreen, taste this ground beef I just fried. Tell me how it is for spiciness."

Nasreen drops the recorder onto her lap, I turn the TV off, and we both slump our shoulders. Before cracking the newspapers open, Nasreen told me she's still mad at her mom, so she doesn't seem thrilled about having her in her room. I'm also down in the dumps because this is the second time I've tried to get a recording of Madonna, but it seems impossible.

"I'm going to step outside," Nasreen says. "After I taste Mom's cooking, I need to check the mail, and maybe I'll walk around the block to clear my head."

"Sure thing." When she leaves, I pull my scrapbook from under my pillow. With scissors, glue, and staples, I add the following items to some fresh pages:

A picture of Madonna I cut out of a newspaper. I want to remind myself I forgot to bring her music on this trip, which has led to a domino effect of problems.

Wahib's business card. Even though the man is obnoxious and wanted to rip us off, I don't want to forget what I had done. My scrapbook contains both the high and low points of my life.

There's also a picture of a dancer in a tutu and leggings I found in a magazine. I've been dying to dance, but I haven't had a chance to so far. I need room, and there doesn't seem to be any inside the basement apartment or even outdoors with the thick crowds of New Yorkers. I also want to be on that show I saw, but Nasreen thinks it's a bad idea. Maybe I'm just not meant to be in the limelight.

***

"What have you seen so far?" my mom asks.

"Oh, you know, the typical places... the Empire State Building, the Statue of Liberty..." I'm lying through my teeth. Nasreen and I are too busy finding a replacement Kulthum tape to do any real sightseeing.

"Lucky girl to see such places."

"Yeah. The Cloisters are beautiful, and I've lost track of the museums I've gone to." When did I become such a liar? I've never lied this much to my mom before.

"Are you careful in the subway? You're not going out at night, are you?"

"No." That's true, I don't go out at night, but I'm not careful in the subway. When I'm out with Nasreen, we check out guys, listen to our Walkmans, and sometimes read a newspaper, unaware of our surroundings. Dad would tell me I'm a mugger's dream.

"What are you doing now?"

"Uncle is going to take me out."

"Have fun. We love you." She smacks her lips together in a loud kiss, and we hang up.

We're going out tonight. I'm not painting the town red... I'm seeing more uncles.

In my family uncles, aunts, and cousins are important parts of our lives. During my vacation time, I'm with at least one of the clans. I've been to Los Angeles, Paris, Toronto, and many other big cities thanks to these family members. My parents don't believe in hotels. I've never stayed in one. We stay with family.

It's a relief my parents aren't here with me now. Not just because I want to be free, but also because years ago we all actually stayed in the basement apartment... for an entire week. Talk about uncomfortable claustrophobia. Nasreen and I shared the bottom bunk. My brothers shared the top bunk. Mom slept on the living room sofa, while Dad slept on the floor next to her. We were packed like sardines in this *sarcophagus*, to borrow Nasreen's term. At least it's just me representing the family, not that I'm doing a great job since I ruined Uncle's tape. But tonight he won't be looking for his tape since we're all going to Uncle Javed's home in Queens.

Omar doesn't feel like going, though. "I don't want to go, Baba," he pleads, his big eyes turning sad in front of Uncle.

"All right, you don't have to go," Uncle says. "Your sister and cousin will come with me, and you can stay here with your mother."

"But I don't want to go either!" Nasreen says, crossing her arms under her chest.

"You are going. I can't go there by myself. They'll think none of you want to visit."

"We don't."

"Stop it, Nasreen. You and Asma are coming with me."

Nasreen's jaw muscles look as taut as violin strings. Omar gets his way, while we young ladies have to do what the menfolk say. We go into her room to change. I don't want anyone looking at my legs and judging me, so I switch to jeans. "You know, a thought just came to me. Maybe this is a good opportunity to look for tapes at Uncle Javed's place," I say.

"Hey, you're right," Nasreen says, her mood brightening. She smiles. "Uncle Javed's cassette collection is just as big as Dad's."

"I can't quite remember where it is," I say.

"I know where to find it," she says. "And it'll be easy getting there. Uncle Javed doesn't breathe down people's necks like Dad does. If he catches us, I'll tell him I'm interested in his collection, and he'll think I'm exploring my roots. Dad doesn't want me looking through his music, but Javed will be happy. My family always complains I'm listening to devil music, so they'll be comforted by me listening to their stuff."

I laugh. My parents also think I listen to devil music. My mom tells me that if I listen to too much radio, it's the same as worshipping Shaitan. I don't even listen to Ozzy or Metallica or anything like that. To my mom, excessive music listening pulls me away from all things religious and spiritual. Music might not be religious, but it is spiritual. I want to sing and dance, but my parents don't allow me to try out for the cheerleading squad or audition for the glee club after hours. I want to see Madonna at Madison Square Garden, but I don't want my uncle to have a heart attack and then call my parents so they can have heart attacks too, because what if I get kidnapped or there's a shootout or stampede or God knows what else at the concert—as if that really happens at every concert.

"Uncle Javed is cool," I agree. "I bet he won't even mind if we dub an Umm Kulthum cassette if we were to find one."

"Absolutely not. I've copied tapes there since he has more stereo equipment than Dad does," Nasreen says. "Okay, so my bratty brother may have gotten out of this one and I didn't really want to go anywhere tonight, but now we have a purpose."

"Yes, a purpose."

"We erased Kulthum, but we'll find her again," Nasreen says, as if we lost an actual person. But considering how people love her and she's Uncle's favorite singer, it's like there's an actual absence in the household. And if Uncle were to find out, he'd mourn over that cassette.

"A Kulthum we will go."

"A Kulthum we will go."

"Hi-ho, the derry-o, A Kulthum we will go..."

"That's enough," Nasreen says, squeezing her eyes shut. "Your voice is making my ears bleed."

"My singing isn't that bad," I say.

Nasreen snorts. Negative girl. But we'll do something positive tonight.

Chapter Ten

I thought I was done with subway rides for the day, but Uncle, Nasreen, and I make the journey to Queens. Sitting on orange and yellow chairs and staring at multiple surfaces covered in graffiti, I jostle against Nasreen and Uncle, who reads *The New York Times*. His fingers are inky from reading newspapers all day. News is his crack-cocaine, what with his newspapers and shortwave radio. We've been fortunate that in the past few evenings he's either been visiting friends or listening to international news on his radio. Maybe he forgot about Umm, or perhaps I overestimated how much he likes her.

"When we get home it'll be late," he says, putting his newspaper in his lap. He smoothes his moustache and yawns.

"Well, we don't have to be making this trip," Nasreen says, barely audible above the chugging wheels of the train

"I'd like to watch TV," I say. Nasreen pokes me in the ribs and I yelp. "I mean, I can't wait to watch TV in the morning, because when we get home it'll be bedtime."

"Yes, we'll all be tired tonight, but before I sleep I'd like to listen to some Umm Kulthum. I only have one complete tape of her beautiful voice. Her voice brings peace."

I close my eyes, the sinking feeling in my heart deepening, but there's a light at the end of the tunnel. Uncle Javed has a stack of music, and we'll be mining through that collection tonight.

Leaving the last subway station makes me breathe a sigh of relief. From basement apartment to the subway, I've been feeling like a mole person lately. I want sunlight and fresh air. The sun is still out in the late evening, and I bask in the glory of a full moon I spot between clouds and buildings. We walk up some porch steps, where Uncle Javed lives in a narrow townhouse. There's the pulsating sound of music from inside the house. When someone opens the door, tabla drums of old-fashioned music reach my ears. I'm not into my parents' music, but I admit some of it makes me want to dance.

Javed welcomes us in. He's tall, tan, and clean-shaven. He's at least ten years younger than Uncle Farhad. He smells of something strange and pungent. Nasreen whispers, "He's been drinking."

He's known to do that. He's into arak and American women. His home is a bachelor pad, which is why I never stay with him when I'm in New York. My parents don't want me and my siblings to see the seedy way he lives, even though I think his lifestyle is cool and normal.

"Is that my little Asma?" he asks.

I hug him, getting a whiff of cologne and whatever he's been drinking. "Yes, it's me."

"*Ma'shallah*, you've grown. Come in!"

"We won't stay long," Uncle says.

"Nonsense. The party has just started."

My parents have unfairly warned me about Uncle Javed. "Seedy" is many friends, laughter, booze, and paintings of half-naked women. Javed is a painter, and on his walls are mermaids, women draped in towels, and ladies in other states of undress. Inside the living room are other aunts and uncles, artist friends, and pretty lady friends. Javed puts his arms around many people, particularly the women. Cigarette smoke drifts around me. I count at least a dozen smokers in the crowded space. I'm sort of used to it since many of my relatives smoke, but back home nobody smokes. I just left the subway, but now I feel like I'm underground again. I desire fresh air.

Uncle glares at Javed with disapproval, yet Javed's licentious ways won't stop him from talking about what he loves the most: current events. "What has happened to Iran?" Uncle asks. "Are you watching the news?"

"And what are you going to do about it?" Javed asks. "All you do is talk. You either go there or do something, or stay here and build a life for your family. It's one or the other."

"You can't ignore what goes on there! The land is in shambles. There's no freedom, just torture and imprisonment."

Some people are mumbling, and others are yelling, bashing Khomeini and the regime of Iran. Javed doesn't want any part of the political talk, walking away from Uncle and slinging his arm around a woman. "Who wants wine?"

Many of my relatives shake their heads. No alky-hol for them. Nasreen eyes the liquor cabinet. I've never seen anything like it; it's an entire piece of furniture dedicated to alcohol, with bottles of amber liquid behind the glass. "Do you think we can score some?" my cousin asks.

"Stay focused," I say. "Let's go find some Umm."

It's a sea of bodies. I thought Uncle's basement apartment was bad, but the fact is most New York homes are small. As I move, random uncles, aunts, and cousins hug and kiss me. Their cigarette smoke clings to me. I smell nicotine-stained skin and lips. I'm afraid of lung cancer and emphysema, not that they're contagious, but the smoky air is ominous. "Someone open a window!" one of the partygoers demands.

As I circulate, my relatives all notice I've grown.

"Such pretty eyes," an aunt says.

"Wow, you're a stunner," an older female cousin named Mahla says. "We'll be looking for a husband for you in no time."

This husband talk makes me more nervous. I grab Nasreen by the arm and pull her through the living room. On our way to Javed's painting room, she grabs something off a table.

"What is that?" I ask.

"A bottle of I don't know what," she says.

"We're not drinking anything."

"To the left," Nasreen directs in the narrow hallway, the bottle still in her hand.

There's a front and back stairwell in Javed's home. The back stairwell will lead us to Javed's painting space, where his music also happens to be. There are cassettes in the living room, but while relatives were grabbing and kissing me, Nasreen looked through them and didn't find any Umm. "Most of his music is up here," she says.

"I hope you're right," I say.

We're on the second floor. There are two bedrooms and Javed converted one of them to his painting space. I turn on a light and I'm confronted by easels, canvas boards, and paints... also, more flesh. There are even nudes propped up against walls.

"Whoa, nice paintings," Nasreen says.

"He's very talented," I say. "But I can see why he keeps this here." Nude paintings are the results of nude models, and I don't want to think about any of my relatives in that light. Nasreen puts the pilfered bottle of wine on a table, and we start looking.

I open a closet and it's full of paint supplies, but we hit it big with the other closet. There's a whole entire shelf dedicated to cassettes. We pull out the boxes, sit on the floor, and look. We don't want to sit on the chairs or sofa because who knows how many naked booties have been on those things.

It looks like the other collections I've seen. Many bootleg cassettes, a few real inserts featuring pictures of the singers, and foreign script I can't read. I put the ones with Arabic and Persian writing to the side since Nasreen is better at reading them than me. We're looking for Umm's name or picture. At least I know how she looks... like a queen with her big hair, stately profile, and luxurious dresses. So far, I haven't seen her image.

"Hey, this may be it," I say, finding a cassette with a picture of an older woman with hair in a large bun, red lipstick, and sunglasses.

"That does look like her!" Nasreen screeches.

"Shhh, keep quiet," I say. There's a bathroom downstairs, as well as one upstairs, but we don't know who may pop in and for what reason. We were going to ask Javed if we could come up here and we were sure he would say yes, but he was too busy arguing with Uncle and following the trail of single women. We don't have his permission to be here but assume he'd be cool about it if he catches us.

Nasreen takes the cassette from my hands. She inspects the outside and then looks inside. "It looks like her," she says. "Oooh, it says 'Umm Kulthum' on the side. This is it."

"This is it," I echo with a sigh. "This is the answer to our problem. We don't have to tell Uncle what really happened, we won't get into trouble, and we won't have to go back to those skeevy men in Brooklyn to fork over one hundred dollars. I'm so relieved."

Nasreen turns around. She's looking at a cassette player next to a can of brushes. "Let's take a listen," she says.

"You're right," I say. "Our initial plan was to dub, not to steal."

"That's right. We're not stealing from Javed. If anyone interrupts us or if Dad says we need to leave soon, then we'll ask Javed if we can borrow this tape, but we must do that secretly or Dad will ask questions. First, I want to be positive this is the tape before we copy it or bring it home. Also, I pretty much memorized the songs on the original tape's insert, and we need to make sure this is a good match."

There she is with her gloomy, skeptical self. I'm positive this is the tape and our search is over. "Okay, but with the party going on downstairs, let's keep the volume low at first before we dub..."

Chapter Eleven

Music shakes the floor. Someone downstairs has turned it up. Drumbeats and a man wailing about romance fill the entire house. I'm in a new world. I'm far from Florida, out of Uncle's house and in another uncle's house, surrounded by strange sights and smells. I've been in New York for a few days, and I've managed to get myself into trouble and all sorts of situations. This isn't me, although I've daydreamed of intrigue and adventure.

I imagine myself back in Miami, in my room listening to pop stars, at the mall with my friends, at school where people know me as the "quiet, athletic girl," and at relatives' houses where I daintily eat pastries and talk about neutral things like soccer, school, and studying. I visit Misty and Tamara's houses to help them pick outfits. We braid each other's hair and paint our nails during weekends of innocent fun. I discuss my grades and what I want to do with my life. Now I find myself doing all sorts of odd things, in various boroughs, during all times of the day, and even in Nasreen's closet. Life isn't about gazing at the TV set wishing I were the characters. There's more to me than my beloved scrapbook.

Javed has a large stereo with two cassette players for dubbing, and Nasreen fumbles with the buttons. "Will you help me with this?" she asks.

"Your eyeliner is running down your face," I gasp.

She puts a hand to her cheek, and black traces of powder stain her fingers. I didn't realize we were both sweating so heavily. I'm used to central air in Miami, but many buildings in New York don't have it. There are air-conditioning units hanging out of windows, or some people go without, relying on open windows in the summer and radiators in the winter. Javed's windows are open, but that's not doing anything to cool me. My bangs, which I had carefully hair-sprayed before I left, are sticking to my forehead, and Nasreen's eyes are a blotchy mess. Instead of the smoky-eye look, it looks like she's sporting two shiners.

"Let's just do our business and get some fresh air," I say. "Javed has a backyard, right?"

"Yes," Nasreen says. "I'm dying for some air. We'll do this and then talk my dad into leaving soon."

I find the On switch and Nasreen hits Play. We wait for the first few seconds of blankness, the part where the tape is white and then it turns into the black strip holding sound. I always itch to hit Fast Forward on that strip, but then I end up going too far ahead.

There's a dramatic beginning with guitars. It almost sounds electronic and modern. This is strange, but Umm made music for years. I'm sure she experimented with different sounds. She died in the seventies. Maybe she even dabbled in disco.

Nasreen rubs at her eyes some more, so now there's black stuff all across her cheeks and forehead. She wipes her hands across her pants. "I can't wait to copy this," she says.

"Shhh," I say. I imagine I'm the Bionic Woman with powerful hearing. I recall the show's sound effects, that eerie echo sound whenever Lindsay Wagner does something extraordinary. My ears are powerful as they listen on, and they hear something dreadful...

A man's voice comes on. He's speaking English, not Arabic.

"Hey, I know this song," Nasreen says.

"Is this Bon Jovi?" I ask.

Nasreen presses Fast Forward. Someone accuses me of giving love a bad name.

"This is Bon Jovi!" my cousin shrieks in surprise.

"Fast Forward some more. There must be some Umm Kulthum songs on this thing."

Nasreen sings along to the next Bon Jovi song. She closes her eyes, the black marks looking ridiculous on her face. "Who-ah..."

"Stop it!" I say. I push Stop and flip the cassette over, but all it has is guitars and male voices. Side B sounds like Van Halen.

"I didn't know Javed was into rock," Nasreen says. "How cool is that?"

"And how much does it suck that this isn't Umm Kulthum?"

"I'm sorry, Asma. Let's keep looking."

As we return to the boxes of cassettes, I make a big stink about our raised, then dashed, hopes. "How could Javed tape over Umm?" I ask.

"Who are we to judge?" Nasreen says. "We did the same."

"That was an accident. We thought it was a blank tape, and we only ruined a few minutes of it. Javed, on the other hand, used the whole thing. That was on purpose. You don't accidentally tape over an entire cassette. Her name is on the cassette and everything."

"If everyone starts taping over Umm, there will be no replacement cassettes for us to find."

"Don't say that. Some people have respect. Even I know she's a great singer." The Madonna of Arabia.

We've exhausted ourselves looking through the boxes. We go through them a second and third time. "Let's just go already," Nasreen says. "My eyes hurt reading the script and fine print."

"What a bummer. I don't want to think about it, but maybe those brothers in Brooklyn are really our only shot at getting these songs."

"I hate thinking about it too, but you're right."

My legs are stiff from sitting for what seems like forever on the floor, and my clothes are sticking to my skin. We get up like old people, our bones creaking, and Nasreen takes the bottle from the table.

"You're putting that back?" I ask.

"Nope," she says.

We go down the back stairwell and into the kitchen. There's a door leading to a garden with a metal security door over it. We also have that in Miami, but not every house has bars over windows and doors. In New York, everything is hard to get into. There are bars, grates, doormen... barriers because the city is big and dangerous. All I want is an Umm Kulthum tape, and a city that's supposed to have everything doesn't have that for me. There's a barrier across that too.

Javed has a tiny yard with a wooden fence that's rickety and missing a few slats. There are plastic chairs facing a small table with an opaque glass top. We sit in the dimly lit yard. Nasreen places the bottle between us. I see that it's red wine. Merlot.

Nasreen wipes her face some more, and there are no longer black marks on her forehead and cheeks; they've transferred to her hands and arms. I still feel icky and moist but considerably better in the outdoors. I inhale deeply, my head tilted to see the full moon. I smell whiffs of barbecue, Chinese food, fish, and whatever else the neighbors are cooking. Not only can I hear Javed's party, but a few doors down I hear someone playing rap music. Despite the noise, I feel peaceful, even though we ran into another problem tonight.

Nasreen pulls a strand of hair to her nose. "I smell like

an ashtray," she says.

I do the same, sniffing my hair. I also smell of cigarette smoke. That was just from being downstairs for a few minutes. Uncle must smell like actual tobacco leaves since he's been inside the whole time. When we get home I'll take a shower, and if Nasreen is up to it we'll watch TV in her closet. I'm in the mood for Letterman.

"You want to take a swig?" Nasreen asks, nodding her head toward the wine bottle.

"No, I shouldn't," I say. "I've never drank before."

"I have. It's no big deal. You should do it."

"No, no." My parents don't have alcohol in the house. My mother has never tasted it, and my father only tried it once, but didn't like the taste. We're not drinkers. Also, TV taught me all about winos on the street who are unkempt and without jobs because they drink all day.

"Come on, Asma," Nasreen says. "Live a little. One sip won't hurt."

But what if guilt consumes me? My few minutes kissing Dorito-breath made me feel bad about myself. I did something against my upbringing, something my parents would disapprove of. Looking at Javed's nude paintings just now felt a little wrong. Even though I'm now wearing makeup and trendy clothes, putting my plain soccer-star self behind me, and even though I think about boys and daydream of having a summer fling, there's something inside me that agrees with my parents and doesn't want them to be ashamed of me.

"Well, I'm going to take a sip," Nasreen says. The cork in the wine bottle is loose, and someone had already drunk a third of the liquid. She uncorks it and tips it over, the wine draining into her mouth.

"Stop," I say. "You're drinking too much."

Nasreen puts the bottle down. "Your turn," she says.

"No."

"Your turn, your turn, your turn."

"Stop! What if someone walks in on us?"

"Javed's guests? Please. My father probably has them all riled up about politics. Once they start talking about that, they don't stop. Take a sip and I'll leave you alone, I promise."

Now I'm reconsidering. She won't pressure me anymore? I just have to take one little sip? I can just let the alcohol touch my tongue or maybe take a pretend sip. I grab hold of the bottle, which to my surprise feels chilled even though it's been out of the fridge for a while.

"You can do it," Nasreen urges.

"You can be such a bully," I say.

I put the bottle to my lips and tip my head back. I tip too far, and the bottle has more wine than I realized. It falls into my mouth and down my throat. I start coughing.

Nasreen laughs. Meanwhile I'm dying. That tasted dreadful. I was hoping it would taste like strong grape juice, but it doesn't. It doesn't matter the type of drink—whiskey, wine, beer, a yummy-looking fruity drink—the actual alcohol is detectable. I've smelled it on others, but now it's inside me.

"Congratulations on no longer being an alcohol virgin," Nasreen says. She takes the bottle and drinks some more.

"I didn't... didn't know you were such a lush," I stammer.

"I drink at my friends' homes. I've never been drunk though. You need to stop taking things so seriously, Asma. People our age drink. It's a given."

Now I've done another thing I never saw myself doing. What will I do next? Skydive? Get a tattoo? Rob a bank? The last one would take care of my problems, because with an endless amount of money I can buy an Umm tape with or without those two sleazy brothers.

"We can always rob a bank," I say aloud.

"What college will want me if I have a record?" Nasreen asks. "But hey, maybe we can try seeing if my father has money. I can always use my allowance later on to pay him back."

"What do you mean, pay him back?"

"Everyone has emergency funds around, right? We can look for my father's. I hope it's more than a hundred so he won't notice a big loss. Then as he pays me my allowance, I'll put the money back. We can go to that store in Brooklyn and pay those crooks for their cassette. We've tried so many stores and we came here tonight. Let's face it; this is a hard-to-find cassette."

"I don't know," I hesitate.

"It'll work," Nasreen says.

Stealing from Uncle? What have I come to? Ruining Uncle's favorite tape, lying about my whereabouts when I'm visiting music stores, nights spent in a closet, looking at nudie paintings, drinking alcohol... what's one more thing? I can add thief to the list.

Chapter Twelve

We luck out. We thought Uncle was in the mood to listen to Umm, but he proclaims how tired he is. "I feel like I've talked forever and that we've been out for an eternity," he says. "I'm going to bed."

It's almost eleven when we arrive home, which is late for a weekday. Omar is up though. As soon as he comes in, he asks Uncle to open the coat closet. Uncle has a skeleton key for this closet, and he opens it to retrieve a cigar box. Omar disappears behind the curtains and returns so his father can lock up the box.

"It's cash," Nasreen whispers to me. "The boy is loaded. I don't know how."

"He must be blackmailing other people besides us," I say.

My eyes are on Uncle's skeleton key attached to the rest of his key ring. He always has his keys on him, and I'm unaware of a duplicate key. I've peeked into the coat closet before. There's a box of jewelry Auntie rarely wears, priceless antiques and pieces from Iran. There are unused electronics, which might sell for a small fortune. Then there's Omar's cigar box, which I imagine is brimming with cash. He even has a rubber band around it to hold it in, so that the money doesn't burst out.

"Did you have a good time with your mother?" Uncle

asks.

"Yeah, and I went to the playground with friends," Omar says. "We played ball until the sun set. Don't worry, though. Reinaldo and Winston walked me home."

"They're nice boys."

Omar smiles. I'm envious of the money he's collected for himself but relieved this is one more night Uncle won't be looking for Umm. Ever since we destroyed the tape, the urgency to replace it dogs us... and we're still aware we have to act fast. He'll want to listen to her eventually.

"Let's watch some TV," Nasreen says.

Letterman's monologue is hilarious. We both chuckle. I want to guffaw. Nasreen sits on her hands, because when she laughs she pounds her hands against the table, floor, or wherever she's sitting. In the closet, we have to be as quiet as possible so no one knows we're here. While we wait for *Josie and the Pussycats*, I write some letters on a legal pad that I'll mail to my soccer friends in Florida. I'm writing to them about how exciting it is to be in New York, but I don't mention the tape, the icky men at the store, or drinking.

Before I go to sleep, I look through my scrapbook. I've placed glue and tape on the windowsill so I don't have to get in and out of bed and disturb Nasreen, who snores underneath me. I take the label of the bottle of Merlot that I had peeled off before we left the party — while Nasreen was talking to cousins, I lingered in the kitchen and peeled it as slowly as I could, but it's still raggedy and torn in places — and glue it inside my scrapbook. I want to remember tonight. Despite not getting what I wanted, I was in good company. I saw far-flung relatives and dabbled in naughtiness with Nasreen.

***

In the morning, a face looms in front of me. I almost scream in surprise. It's Nasreen. She's perched on the side of the bunk bed staring at me at eye level... without makeup. She looks like a different person, unrecognizable without the eyeliner and shadow smeared across top and bottom lids. Even though I've seen her without makeup before, I thought someone had broken into the apartment.

"What is it?" I ask, rubbing my eyes. "What time is it?"

"It's seven o'clock," she whispers. "My dad is already up getting ready for work. We need to watch my family closely so we can search the apartment and get money. I'll also need my mother and Omar out of the way, but I think I have a plan."

I remember our plans from last night and the drinking I shouldn't have done. Nasreen normally takes showers in the morning, while I take them at night. She still smells like last night's cigarette smoke.

"You stink," I say.

"Thanks, dragon breath. I'll jump into the shower before my dad gets there."

She's done in ten minutes, and she's drying her hair, the blow-dryer loud in the quiet of the morning. Then she begins to paint her face, brushes and sponges in hand as she layers the war paint across her eyes.

The silence of the morning doesn't last because rush hour is building up. I watch calves and torsos glide past me. I used to feel bitter about people-watching. I always imagined others were living better lives than me, doing funner things. I used to look at people, thinking about how they'd shop for more things compared to me — that they laughed more, went to exciting places without relatives, and experienced things I may never go through. Now I realize I'm just as capable of having these adventures, even if they begin the wrong way — by erasing a tape of Uncle's most beloved singer.

I watch Auntie blow Uncle. Okay, that thought came out wrong. What I meant is that Auntie says her prayers, blowing a circle of air around and around Uncle's face. This will protect him from muggers and stabbers on his subway ride to work. If we go out today, she'll do the same to us. Blow and blow.

"Don't forget your prayer pouch," Auntie says. She hands Uncle a triangular pouch, which looks identical to the one I saw with Nasreen days ago. It has papers inscribed with prayers sewn into it.

"Your mom sure is religious," I say.

"And superstitious," Nasreen says. She pulls a necklace from under her t-shirt and shows me an evil-eye bead. The evil eye. When I was a child, my mom would go on about it as if it were real. I would dream about a huge, evil-looking eye gliding across the floor to hunt me down with promises of danger and disease.

With Uncle out of the way, we both go into the bathroom. We squeeze into it, our elbows jostling each other as we style our hair. We use so much Aqua Net spray that the bathroom reeks of its scent. The ozone layer is suffering because of us.

My bangs are swept up into a wave, while Nasreen's hair spikes up like scissors, her favorite style. We go to the kitchen, where Omar and Auntie are eating breakfast.

"Come eat this cheese," Auntie says. "It's so delicious. I need to buy some more soon."

I pick up a piece of bread and put a slice of cheese on it. It tastes like Monterey Jack. Nasreen doesn't pick at the food. "Are you going shopping today?" she asks.

"Today or tomorrow," Auntie says.

"I'm almost out of hairspray," Nasreen says. This is true. We use a lot of it.

"That's not important," Auntie says, patting a piece of bread with a spoonful of yogurt. "You can wait an extra day for that."

"And I need some pens and pencils."

"I just went to your room. You have a cup of pens on your desk."

"Let's go to the toy store!" Omar says. Gross. His mouth is full of fruit and he's talking.

"Whatever you like, my little fellow," Auntie says, changing her tune. "I suppose I can shop today, not tomorrow."

I look at Nasreen but see no change in her. I'm upset for her. How horrible that Omar is the favorite child and whatever he says goes! At least Auntie will be out of the apartment soon so we can look for money.

We watch morning news and entertainment shows in the living room, waiting for the two of them to leave. Shopping for Uncle and Auntie is different from how we shop in Miami. In Miami my parents jump into a car and ride from shopping complex to shopping complex to get things on their list. It might take a long time depending on how many stops they make and what the traffic's like.

In New York, when I've shopped with Auntie, she walks long blocks. She bargain-shops. If another store has something for a dime cheaper, then a dime cheaper it is, and she's off to another store. She once took me clothes shopping, and it was interesting seeing how she measures things. She takes her thumb and forefinger, spread apart, and uses that length as a ruler. Her two fingers glide across clothes to measure them. I know my waist is two thumb-forefinger spans, while Nasreen's is slightly bigger by a thumbnail. After measuring clothes, my aunt inspects every inch for tears and other aberrations. Shopping with her takes forever, so I avoid doing so.

"Would you like to come with us?" Auntie asks.

"No," we say simultaneously. I don't want her to finger-measure any clothes and I have to be here for my first foray in thievery.

Sitting on a sofa watching *Regis and Kathie Lee*, Nasreen crosses her legs, while I fold mine under myself or otherwise I'd be tapping my feet nervously. Omar walks by. He narrows his eyes.

"What do you want?" Nasreen asks.

"You two are up to something," he says.

"And you aren't? All you do is spy on people."

"Me? Spy? Something about you two is off, and I'm going to find out what it is."

"Get out of here. Go behind your curtain, you little troll."

He sticks his tongue out and disappears, his green curtains flapping behind him. Ever since that area was sectioned off, I've never been behind those curtains.

"Do you think there's a chance we can open that closet and get to Omar's money?" I whisper. "It'll only be fair since some of it is ours."

Nasreen gives me a sideways glance. "Are you crazy? If anything goes missing, he'll know we're behind it. We have a motive since he recently blackmailed us. Anyway, only Dad and the super have the key to that closet."

My hopes regarding the coat closet and Omar's cigar box are dashed. An hour later Auntie and Omar are by the front door, dressed for their outing. She's wearing a lavender dress, and he's wearing shorts and a Spiderman t-shirt. She blows her holy wind on him and says a prayer. I realize that while she blows on everyone, no one blows on her. Who will pray for Auntie's safety?

Omar bends down to tie a shoelace when I notice something disturbing. There are two white patches on each side of his head. Typically, on people with short hair, I notice one whorl, where the hair has a natural pattern of growth spiraling from the middle of the head. Omar doesn't have one whorl but two.

I nudge Nasreen's ribs. "Take a look at that," I say.

"Devil's horns," she whispers.

My mom told me that people with two whorls represent the devil, because that's where horns grow. Here

Auntie is so superstitious, taking heed of everything from the old country, but she never mentions that her own son has the markings of Satan. It doesn't surprise me. At least he'll be out of our way for a few hours and the apartment will be a demon-free zone during that time.

***

"Okay, they're gone," Nasreen says, leaping off the couch. "Let's start looking. Just make sure you put things back exactly as you found them."

"Will do."

Nasreen is twice as fast as I am. It's her home, after all. She looks through her parent's room and living room, finding four dollars worth of loose change. I try the closet door in the front hallway to make sure it's locked, still thinking of that box of money, but Uncle hasn't left it open. Then I'm in the kitchen, putting utensils and appliances back where I found them, handling them with care since I'm afraid Auntie will notice something's awry. When I reach the last drawer, I hit pay dirt.

There's a list, but it's in Persian. It's paper-clipped to six ten dollar bills. Sixty dollars! It's not the one hundred we're looking for, but it's something.

"Nasreen, I found something!" I say.

She rushes over and smiles. "This looks like an old shopping list for groceries, sewing stuff, and school supplies," she says. "I think it's from September. Mom must have forgotten about it."

"Yeah, or she would have taken it with her just now."

"According to what you say you have left over for your trip expenses and considering that Omar fleeced me, we don't have one hundred dollars, but maybe if we go back to the store in Brooklyn the guy can lower the price or we can haggle. Maybe he'll drop the price to seventy-five or eighty."

"But what if your mom notices today or tomorrow that the money's missing?"

"I don't think she'll notice anytime soon since it's been here awhile. Also, in a few weeks I can replenish it. Aunt Latifah is visiting from Buffalo in August, and she always gives me money when she comes down here. Also, I won't spend a dime of my allowance."

"Still, a few weeks is a long time."

"Not for my mom," Nasreen says. "She won't notice it missing right away. Anyway, if she sees something is gone, she blames jinn. You know, genies? She says they move stuff to cause mischief."

My parents have warned me about jinn, that they shift things around people's homes as a prank. Shortly before I left, my mother lost her sewing kit and blamed it on them. "In that, case, let's go to Brooklyn, and I'm sure the store owner can't turn this money down," I say. "Let's go today."

"We'll wait for Mom to come back so I can tell her we're sightseeing." She says the last word with air quotes. It's okay since I've seen all of New York's biggest sights during previous trips. Right now my mind is on the replacement tape.

"But, maybe there is more money somewhere," I say.

"We've checked every room. I even checked the toilet tank, because people keep things in there to hide from burglars."

"Yuck."

"I checked my dad's desk in the living room. Really, there's just the closet."

"You're forgetting one place. I know you said we can't take from him, but at least we can take a peek behind Omar's curtains."

Nasreen's eyes darken. I also feel a bit ill thinking about it. Those curtains have come to symbolize something mysterious and sinister, but I'm still curious. What's behind those curtains? What does Omar do for hours a day behind them?

"All right," Nasreen says. "Things are so rocky between me and him that I haven't been there in months."

"Really?" I say.

"Yeah. Let's go though."

Nasreen follows me. When something pokes my back, I jump up and yelp. She laughs at my fear. "Oooh, the boogeyman will get you," Nasreen howls in a spooky voice. "Boooogeyman."

"I don't expect rainbows and butterflies, but I know we're bound to see something frightening in there."

"You first," she says.

"No, you," I say.

"No... you!"

"All right, all right, I'll go first."

Chapter Thirteen

The curtains are emerald green and shimmery. In my opinion, they're too good for Omar. He should be living behind flaps of burlap or something. Auntie hand-sews many things, and looking at the stitches they look like they're her work. Not that her sewing is bad or anything, but I can tell the stitches aren't from a machine. The fabric is something she probably purchased during bargain shopping, and it's good quality. She got the best for the prince of the household.

Nasreen stands behind me, humming the theme song for *Jaws*. I grab the curtains and yank them apart. Nasreen stops humming to gasp. The alcove joins the living room, but it's two thirds of the width. So much stuff is crammed inside that small space. The rest of the apartment is cramped, with every inch of closet and drawer space used, but this is something else.

There's a sofa, desk, TV, Atari, Nintendo, boom box, and dresser. I guess Omar can move around in here because he's a little kid, but when Nasreen and I step in it's a small fit.

"How does anyone stay here for hours a day?" I ask.

"He has everything he needs," Nasreen says, picking up a Nintendo cartridge. She studies the cover and then throws it back down with the rest of the pile on the floor. "Everything that's important to him is here. Anyway, you see how he's always going to the playground with friends. It's not like he's here all the time."

"Still..."

The sofa is unmade, with a blanket scrunched up and a pillow indented with the shape of Omar's head on the other end. Nasreen sits down, while I'm on my knees on the floor. She turns to the side, leaning forward to look through his dresser. There are clothes, candy, and toys in there. Everything is a disorganized mess. If Nasreen's room looked like this, Uncle and Auntie would rag on her, but Omar can get away with sloppiness.

I sit on the carpet and see some things stacked underneath the sofa. It looks like Omar's classwork from the school year that just ended. There are math equations, grammar, As, and Bs. He seems like a good student. And based on how Uncle and Auntie treat him, he's the perfect son. Too bad he sucks as a brother and a cousin.

I flip through the next notebook. This is different from the others. Omar hasn't labeled it with his name or a subject area. Each page has a list on it.

Handball Teams
Team 1: Reinaldo, Jesse, Omar, Freddy, Haider
Team 2: Chris, Luke, Mike, Winston, Hector
Winner: Team 1, $20

I flip through the pages and see the same thing on each of them. Sometimes instead of "handball," I see "cards" or "basketball." The winning teams win anywhere from ten to thirty dollars, with each list having three to six players each.

"Nasreen, check this out," I say.

"What's this?" she asks when I put the notebook in her lap.

"It looks like your brother is partaking in some gambling."

"What?" She flips through the pages, her mouth forming an *O*.

"It's quite lucrative," I say. "They must pool the money and then split it, and Omar is on many of the winning teams.

This goes on for pages and pages. He must've been doing this for months."

"That little shit!" Nasreen yells. "We can't even afford the tape from that asshole in Brooklyn, and one of the reasons is because we gave money to Omar to keep quiet so he doesn't tell my dad we were using his stereo, when he doesn't need the money. He's making plenty of dough! That's why he's always begging to go out to the corner playground to play with the neighborhood kids. This is why he's always asking Dad to take the cigar box out of the coat closet, because that's where he's saving his money. He must lie to Dad and say he's saving his allowance, Ramadan money, and family gifts. No, he's getting most of his money by doing this!"

"I wouldn't doubt he's the brainchild of this operation," I say. "Your brother is greedy and has brains, although he uses his intelligence for evil."

"Yeah. And if you notice, his friends are the ones who seek him out. If he doesn't come out, they're knocking on our door, so polite to my parents and asking them if Omar can come out and play."

"Yes, I've noticed."

Nasreen puts the notebook on the arm of the sofa. "We need to make a copy of this gambling diary."

"How?" I wonder. "If we take this for photocopies, Omar will notice it's missing."

"Go get my camera," she says. "I'll set up here."

I know where her camera bag is. It's hanging off a nail in her closet, above the TV she's not supposed to be watching late at night. When I bring it to her, she opens it and takes out the Kodak camera. "We're ready," she says.

It feels like we're in the secret police. This is what spies must do in Iran. I'm always hearing about police and spy activity, cloak-and-dagger stuff, torture rooms, abductions, and political intrigue. Nasreen and I don't keep up with what's going on in the old country since we're part of this new country, but we listen to our parents go on about spies and family friends who sell information. Sure, this only involves my cousin and gambling on the playground, but it still feels exciting and wrong—in the right way since Omar deserves being found out like this. He holds things over others, so we'll hold something over him.

Nasreen turns on the alcove light since there are no windows and the meager light from the living room doesn't reach this area. Then she stands on the couch at an awkward angle, slightly bent over, while the notebook is on the floor. She can't do close-ups because the camera manual doesn't suggest it. I flip the page, getting out of the way as she snaps. I flip, she snaps, until we've taken a picture of many of the pages. Nasreen doesn't have enough shots for the whole book since Omar has been gambling for quite a while.

"We're done," Nasreen says.

"So how will we use these pictures?" I ask.

"My parents think the world of Omar. They think he's heaven-sent. What a joke. We'll have to use these at the right time and really threaten him, or else he'll give my parents some bullshit lie that this notebook was for math class or that he was only gambling in monopoly money."

"Yes, we'll have to be careful." He's only eight, but we're talking about him as if he's a mafia kingpin—he's as wily as one, though.

"My film has one last picture left."

"Let's get someone to take our picture!" I say.

"Good idea," Nasreen agrees. I don't want Auntie and Uncle to take any more pictures of me. I can't forget our picture-taking experience a few days ago, when I felt like I was taking mug shots rather than family pictures.

We both step outside and approach a cute guy who's hailing a cab. When the cab zooms past him, ignoring him, we ask him to take our picture.

"Anything for you two beautiful ladies," he says in a

deep voice. He has a sexy radio voice. I've heard the joke that people with a radio voice have a face for radio, but he's an exception to this belief.

I giggle and Nasreen smiles, putting her guard down. She hands him her camera. We put our arms around each other, my lime-green shoulder against her black shirt, and my straight hair against her prickly spikes. We smush our cheeks together and smile wide. Auntie and Uncle would disapprove of this pose, calling it childish and improper, but they're not here.

Click.

***

The guy is gorgeous. He has thick, black lashes, cheekbones, a jawline that could cut glass, and muscles straining against his sleeves. He chats after he takes our picture. He tells us he's a student at NYU studying archeology. Ooh, an older man. Nasreen and I are glued to the sidewalk. When another cab comes his way, he manages to get it. "Sorry, ladies, but I'm late for an appointment," he says. "Thanks for keeping me company."

When he's inside the cab, he blows me a kiss. Or does he blow Nasreen a kiss? "My heart is melting," I say.

"We have to go back," Nasreen says, looking at her Swatch.

I look at my own Swatch, and I'm startled by the time. It really flies by when you're snooping and doing things you're not supposed to be doing.

We get back inside. Nasreen puts her camera bag away. I put the notebooks back under the sofa the way I found them, or how I remember I found them. Math, science, and English... then the gambling notebook at the very bottom. Nasreen had disturbed some of Omar's toys, so she sets Transformers and Gobots upright.

We step out of the alcove. I put my hands back on the curtains to draw them shut. There's a problem. The right side is snagging against the curtain rod. I pull, but it won't budge.

"What's wrong?" Nasreen asks, joining me in the yanking.

"I don't know," I say.

"Hurry up." Her efforts are also futile, because the curtain panel refuses to be drawn shut.

Then we hear the jingle of keys as someone opens the door. This can't be happening, not when we've done our best to cover our tracks.

Chapter Fourteen

Here's another difference between New York and Miami: the complexity of key chains. I have one key for my front door, but Uncle and Auntie have multiple keys.

They have the key to the lobby to get their mail and throw garbage down a chute, a key to their mailbox, and three keys for the front door. Omar's voice booms behind the door. "Come on, Mom! I need to pee."

The second lock twists open. Nasreen pulls her father's desk chair to her, hops onto it, and lifts the curtain to unsnag it from the bump in the rod.

"Help me," she says.

I pull and it moves. The curtains are closed! Nasreen shoves the chair back to her father's work area, where books and bills are in piles. Then we throw ourselves onto the sofa, as if everything's normal. We're two cousins who spent the morning chatting.

Auntie's working on the third lock. I'm breathless but force myself to slow down my breathing. Three seconds inhale, three seconds exhale. Omar rushes past me to the bathroom, and Auntie comes in, putting paper and plastic bags on the kitchen counter.

Nasreen and I help Auntie put things away. Omar saunters out of the bathroom and heads to the bags that contain new toys. He's truly a prince, getting everything he wants at home and then handling an underground economy at the yard where he plays with his friends.

My cousin goes to her room to look through brochures of colleges her parents won't let her attend. I continue sitting on the sofa, pondering my dilemmas: I want to go to the Madonna concert, but the more pressing issue is replacing the Kulthum tape. Omar hums a happy tune as he walks through his curtains, disappearing into his haven of toys and games.

Since we've put everything away, Auntie wipes the windows; phase one of her housekeeping. When she pulls the curtains open, I'm back to seeing people's legs and torsos cut through the air in a headless world. It adds to the Bizarro quality of my summer vacation.

Auntie has a spray bottle and a towel in hand. I ask her if she needs help. "No, no, you relax," she says.

"Hmmm, that spray smells interesting," I say. It smells sharp, but not like the chemicals I normally detect in household cleaners.

"I mixed it myself," Auntie says, huffing and puffing after her arms get a workout. She puts her hand down, the towel drooping from her fingertips. "It saves money. Anyway, your auntie was once a chemist."

"You were a chemist?" I gasp.

"Yes." She nods. "I have my degree in chemistry and I worked in a lab before I got married."

We look at each other, and I'm falling into confusion and disbelief. Auntie has a science degree? I assumed she was a simple village girl, uneducated, forever destined to be a housewife... but I'm wrong.

Auntie breaks away from my stare and continues to clean. "But I'd rather be here doing this," she says. "This is my home, this is my life. It was exciting going to college and working, but marriage changed me."

"I don't think Nasreen wants to be a housewife," I say. "Or maybe not in the near future."

"I know she wants to leave us," she says. "That's what young people want to do. But I can't let her go that easily, and I want to look out for her safety."

So Auntie had a life, an education, and even a career before she got married. Why doesn't she want the same for her daughter? Why can't Nasreen experience freedom, explore college options and such? I see a chink in the family's armor. Maybe I can persuade Auntie to let Nasreen go to the college of her choice, which will then sway Uncle. I just need to think of how to do this since it won't be easy.

***

Nasreen wants to be super careful with the money. She wears her purse strap across her chest and then throws a denim vest over it. "I've never been mugged, and I want it to stay that way," she says. "We can't lose this money. Let's go."

"I'll cross my fingers that this guy will lower the price."

Auntie blows on us. Spittle lands on my cheeks and nose, which happens sometimes. My parents' voices echo in my head — I shouldn't travel far from Manhattan, be careful in the subway, and don't talk to strangers. But I will talk to strangers: those sleazy men at the Brooklyn store, Wahib and Tahir. I don't like how Tahir looks at me, and Wahib wants to rob us for a tape from his personal collection.

"Hey, can you check the mail and see if there's anything for me?" I ask.

"Sure," Nasreen says. I step inside the lobby with her. Inside there are rows of copper-colored mailboxes with air holes. It's sort of like being in a sci-fi movie, as if these mailboxes contain electronics or maybe alien pods. The mailboxes in Miami, lined up one per house, are so humdrum compared to these. The lobby has a lived-in, comfy smell, like my favorite leather jacket. Nasreen checks the mail, but there are two bills and some junk mail that she leaves inside for her dad.

"Nothing for me?" I ask.

"No." She shakes her head.

"Shoot!"

"Did you expect something from close friends?'

"Yes, or I thought they were close."

"I'm sure they have their own summer plans. You'll catch up with them later."

But they're both at home with no special plans, or so they told me. Tamara and Misty promised they would write to me. I feel jilted and ignored, but I squash down these unpleasant emotions. I'm in the greatest city on the planet, even though I messed up my trip with the Kulthum tape. Once we find a replacement, I'll really enjoy this trip and see what I want to see.

After my disappointment over the mail, we're out on the street. Long train rides ensue, made longer by the first train being stuck in a tunnel for ten minutes. I brought a Harlequin romance book with me, a thin paperback that fits into my purse, and Nasreen has her Walkman, but all we do is end up talking to each other. On our last transfer, we voice our concerns about the tape and the store manager.

"You need to be tough," Nasreen says. "They're going to try to trick us, raise the price, but we need to haggle. Don't let on that we're desperate for the tape, and don't be too nice. They already know we want the tape, but we need to be cooler about it. And you have 'tourist' written all over you. You're too polite and wide-eyed, taking everything in as if you've never been to the big city before."

"That's not true," I say.

"Look, I'm just telling you what I've noticed."

"Okay."

"Okay is not good enough! I'm serious, Asma. You have that open look in your eyes when you need to be guarded. Don't slip and get emotional, because you can't be like that around these people. Trust me that those two men are vultures, ogling us and wanting a ton of money for a tape."

"Okay."

"Ugh! Stop saying okay. You're not making me feel better. I hope you don't mess up."

I don't know why Nasreen thinks I'm going to mess up. Sure I live in the suburbs, have straight As, hang out with other straight-A students, and most of my friends are from my soccer team. All this does shelter me from all the bad kids. I may never have cut class or gone all the way with a boy, but I know there's something inside of me that's street smart and hip. I just wish that side came out of me. I saw an inkling of my wild side when I gussied myself up on the plane ride and talked to Abe, but that's just appearances and a bit of flirtation. I think about Madonna strutting around in the "Papa Don't Preach" video. Her attitude shines through her every motion. I want attitude. I pull my chin up to practice being bad. I give a dirty look to a model in a subway poster. She's advertising a popular perfume. Someone spray-painted nipples on her dress, the black points like eyes, and there's also a red moustache on her.

"What's wrong with your face?" Nasreen asks. "You look like you ate something sour."

I stop trying to look tough. I can't be snappy and snazzy like my favorite idols.

We're here. I don't know my way around Brooklyn since I don't spend much time in that borough, but I remember the way from our previous trip. Straight down and make a right. We're at the store.

"Remember, keep your cool," Nasreen says, her hand on the door. "We can't get nervous."

"Excuse me!" a man says, opening the door and almost knocking us down. He pulls his baseball cap down, ducks his face into the collar of his shirt, and holds a brown paper bag tightly to his chest. The rectangular shape makes it obvious it's a videotape.

"Jerk," Nasreen says. "Come on."

Inside the store, the curtain in the back of the store sways. Another man departs. He's tall and lanky, as well as sweaty and creepy. He smiles at us. Like the guy who bumped into us, he has a paper bag in his hand with a rectangular lump inside.

"I thought there was an office behind those curtains," Nasreen whispers to me.

"I thought so too," I whisper back. "Maybe they do some of their business there."

"Hmmm."

The tall guy leaves, but not before he undresses us with his eyes. They rake over my body in slow motion, as if he's taking off each article of my clothing one by one.

"Okay, I feel naked," Nasreen says.

"Let's be fast and get out of here. This place is full of creeps."

"Hello there!" Wahib says. Closely behind him is his brother, Tahir. Their big bellies emerge first from the curtains, followed by their ridiculous comb-overs.

"Hello," we say.

"Ah, you two are back, Shireen and Isma," he says, which jogs my memory that we gave him fake names. "Are you here for the Umm Kulthum tape?"

"We're wondering if we can strike a deal," Nasreen says.

"I like to stick to my prices, but I don't mind giving a discount now and then. The thing is, it's the only Umm Kulthum tape I have, and I already told you why it's hard for me to part with it. It's not part of the store inventory. This is my tape. Weeks ago I had several of her tapes on the shelves, but they went quickly. It's going to take me a while to get more."

But we don't have a while to get a replacement tape! He doesn't have to be such a jerk because he has this one tape. "Then there shouldn't be a problem if more are coming in," I say.

"But I don't know exactly when," he says. "So for the one I have, it's still one hundred."

"Fifty," Nasreen says.

"One hundred," he says with a smile.

"Fifty-five."

"One hundred." His smile is unwavering.

"Sixty."

"One hundred." The smile plastered on his face fills me with unease.

"Sixty-five."

"Listen, how about a real deal?"

"What do you mean?" I say.

"How old are you two?" he asks.

"Seventeen," I say.

"Eighteen," Nasreen says at the same time. We each made ourselves a year older.

"Interesting," he says. I don't like the sound of this. Anytime a man asks me how old I am, it's never any good. I recall icky men at the mall, at stores, all over the place asking about age. Usually I just walk away, but I feel enclosed in this store, needing something from this man. "How old are you?" men wonder about young girls. "Are you legal?" they're really asking.

"Then you're of age," he says, nodding in Nasreen's direction. Then he looks at me. "Well, you're almost of age." He points to me, the younger one, the seventeen-year-old who's really sixteen.

"Of age for what?" I say, my voice becoming squeaky. Damn, what street-smart person has a squeaky voice? I deepen my voice and ask, "Why is my age important when all we want is this tape?"

"We want something from you," Wahib says. Not only is he the store manager, but he's the big talker of the two. Tahir smiles and rubs his mustache.

"What do you want?" Nasreen asks.

"We want her," Tahir says, breaking his silence, pointing at me. "We want her..."

Chapter Fifteen

"Yes, I want her," Tahir repeats.

There are times when life seems surreal and I wonder if I'm dreaming. Or maybe I'm psychotic and imagining things. Am I really in a store that smells like hair gel—for the brothers' comb-overs, I assume? Am I truly facing two strange men in a small store off the beaten path, away from any major landmarks when I'm in the most exciting city on the planet? I must have entered a parallel universe or something. I know... I must be on *Candid Camera*. But the store is so small that I doubt a camera crew can be hiding somewhere.

"Excuse me?" Nasreen says.

"You want me?" I ask.

"Yes, my brother and I were pondering over matters since we saw you days back," Wahib says. "You see, I came to this country ten years ago, and my situation is settled. But my brother, Tahir you see behind me, he is having problems."

Tahir smiles at me, one of those lopsided smiles that's supposed to be sexy. Yeah, sexy on John Stamos but gross on him!

"What problems?" Nasreen asks.

"And what do his problems have to do with me?" I ask.

"What's your point?" Nasreen snarls. "We came here for a tape, and now you're mentioning your brother. We're not asking about your personal lives. We're customers!"

"Young lady, you have not purchased anything from me, and I'm not done with my story," Wahib oozes, maintaining his cool. He gives us a conciliatory smile, but dread continues to creep up my spine and tension builds across my shoulders. Between the heat and my nerves, I feel faint.

"Anyway," he continues, "my brother is having green card issues. We were thinking that here we are in a country full of strangers, but there are so many nice Middle Eastern girls we can find, many of whom are already citizens. We are a small community in a big city. I see the same customers from Manhattan, Staten Island, even New Jersey, Connecticut. So we were thinking, since you're seventeen and one year away from marrying—"

"Hell no!" Nasreen yells.

"What are you talking about?" I say. "You're talking marriage?" I may want to be grown-up, but I'm still a kid. I also want to find someone on my own, and certainly not some old guy who must have twenty years over me. Tahir rubs his potbelly while Wahib wipes his sweaty forehead with a handkerchief.

"We're not talking marriage," Wahib says. "How about just one meeting to see how the two of you get along?"

"No," I say. "I'm not going to be set up for either a date or marriage."

"We'll get the hundred dollars," Nasreen says, her voice ice-cold. "It still is one hundred, right?"

"The price of my personal tape will not change." He loves repeating that. I bet he'd still have done this to us if the tape were on the shelves. "It's still one hundred, but I'd rather you think my proposition over."

"I'm not trading myself for a tape," I say. As if I'm a hooker or something! How dare they?

"Let's get out of here," Nasreen says. "And we'll definitely come back soon with the money."

"We already have your phone number to alert you of any new tapes coming in," Wahib says.

I feel ill thinking that Nasreen gave them her number, but then I remember she had given them the number of the payphone by her window. I want to get out of here so they can't feast on me with their eyes and words. They just want my hand in marriage, not to do any real business with me. Maybe this was their plan all along. They figured I'm young and probably don't have a hundred dollars to spare, so they had to lure me in for their icky request.

We can't get out of here fast enough. I trip on an uneven patch of the sidewalk, twisting my ankle, and Nasreen bangs her knee against a fire hydrant. "Ouch," she says.

I grab her arm, and we hobble to the corner, away from the windows of Wahib and Tahir's store. I put my weight on my ankle. It hurts, but I don't think it's sprained. "Are you okay?" I ask.

"My knee will be all right," Nasreen says, her face pinched in a grimace. "What about you?"

"My ankle is already feeling better, but it kind of hurts when I walk."

"It would be nice to get a brand new Kulthum tape, instead of their bootleg, but who knows how long that'll take to ship. Anyway, it's not about them trying to get something for a customer. They want your sweet, young ass. Tahir has been drooling over you since you first stepped foot in there, and he probably figured you were born here from the way you talk and dress."

"What if they call us?"

"If they do call the payphone for whatever reason, I figure I can always tell my parents I'm taking out the garbage, checking the mail, or checking up on Omar on the playground. I can be fast enough to catch the ringing phone. If not, I'll just say we have no answering machine. The fact is, so far this is the only tape we've found. It's not like I have a catalog I can purchase this from, and we haven't seen this in any other store. They have the upper hand."

"And they sure know it. We need to get our hands on more money. Uncle is bound to find out the tape is missing for good."

"How are we going to get the rest of the hundred dollars to get this tape? And fast?"

"I think I have an idea," I say.

***

Back home we watch Omar ask Auntie if he can go outside to the corner park to "play" with his friends. As if on cue, there's a knock on his door. It's his friend Scott, a lanky boy with freckles and stick-straight black hair. "Can Omar come out and play?" he asks Auntie.

"Omar, go with your friend," she says, smiling at the two boys.

Nasreen shakes her head. Omar and Scott are acting all sugary and innocent—they eat the cookies Auntie offers them—but they'll be gambling soon. Everyone has money but us, it seems. Sure, we borrowed Auntie's money, but we didn't get to spend it. We need a full payment of one hundred dollars. Haggling didn't work, and those two disturbing brothers wanted me. Tahir desires to have me as a wife so he can stay in the country. And all for a tape. I'm worth a cassette tape. How insulting is that? As if I'm in the old country where women are traded off for livestock and other goods!

"TV, now," I say when Auntie is in the kitchen and out of earshot.

"You want to watch TV?" Nasreen asks. "We need to find the means to get some money."

"And I have an idea."

We're in her room, watching soaps on her regular TV, not her closet TV. Women are crying, men are scheming, and couples are kissing. Then I catch the commercial again, the one for *NYC Dance Off*. "I'm going to enter that," I say. "They have daily cash prizes if you dance on camera."

"Uhhh, I'm pretty sure your parents will be pissed off if they see their daughter on TV," Nasreen says. "And do you dance that well?"

"I sure do. Next to soccer, dancing is my specialty. You need to see me in action. Since they also accept singers, maybe I can try out for that too."

"You sing?" Nasreen asks.

"I enjoy it, but I know I need more practice. Dancing is more my thing, but I can try out for both."

"I don't know about this."

"I'll do my hair and makeup so nobody recognizes me." I imagine seeing myself made up in red lipstick, blue eye shadow, and a sequined dress, the opposite of my soccer persona. No one will recognize me. I think about all the TV shows and movies I've seen where that happens—Wonder Woman takes off her glasses and pulls her hair out of a bun, and she's someone else. I won't look like my same old self for that show.

"I guess we can try it," Nasreen says. "We have nothing to lose."

The commercial comes on a second time. I grab a notepad and pen off Nasreen's desk, spilling a few brochures onto the floor, and write down the toll-free number. There's only one phone in the living room. Ah, I miss my own phone in my bedroom in Miami. I'm going to have to use the payphone outside since I can't reveal my plans to Auntie.

She's busy in the kitchen, so I step out without having to explain my actions to her—she's nosy and always wondering what everyone is up to; meanwhile, she needs to be in Omar's business, not ours. Gambling is against our religion and far worse than what I'm doing.

I wait for a young woman with sky-high bangs and red pumps to get off the phone. Good, she's quick and hangs up. I'm next. I dial the number and get through right away to a secretary. I pump her for information. I write down the address. No appointment is necessary. They have auditions tomorrow starting at ten in the morning. I'll be there.

When I hang up, I stand still, taking in what I did. I'm actually going to try out for a spot on TV. National TV. As in everyone might see me. Money is involved. Dancers are even eligible to get Madonna concert tickets. Maybe I can kill two birds with one stone: get the one hundred dollars and Kulthum tape and see my idol live in concert. A girl can always dream.

Since I'm out here, I decide to call Misty. I brace myself for the automated messages from the operator. I will not get mad, I will not get mad, I will not get mad...

"Hey, buddy," Misty says in her husky voice. "So you finally decided to call me."

"I called Tamara awhile ago, but it's a real pain to make long-distance calls," I say, feeling the need to apologize to her. "I did send you a letter."

"Oh, haven't seen it yet. Tamara mentioned you met a guy. Well, it's about time you get some action."

"Yeah..." Okay, I know I'm not an expert in the love-and-sex department, but she doesn't have to rub it in.

"So what are you doing today? Going to the library? To the park to play some soccer?"

"Of course not," I say. "I'm on vacation."

"I didn't think you'd break out of your routine."

Is this how my friends view me? As some stick-in-the-mud homebody with no life? If only they could see me now, truly experiencing the dangers of New York and its strangers, of being in a boatload of trouble and doing a lot of legwork to get out of it.

"For your information, I'm out of my routine," I say.

Please deposit twenty-five cents.

"What were you saying?" Misty says. "You're returning some library books?"

Please deposit twenty-five cents.

My hand is stuck in my pocket, and I wrench it out, quarter in hand. I deposit it before I lose the call.

"Are you running a few laps this afternoon?" Misty asks. "Don't forget a bottle of water and your vitamins."

"Actually, I'm doing something you'd never believe. There's a show called *NYC Dance Off*..."

"Oh, I love that show! So you watch it too."

"You're not listening!" I say, finally losing my temper.

"I know that show is hot, and so are the dancers."

"I'm going tomorrow."

"Of course, you can be one of those people standing outside the windows watching them live."

There are windows looking out on the street where passersby stand and watch, but she doesn't let me get a word in. I want to be part of the show, and with my dancing skills I know I can make it.

Please deposit twenty-five cents.

"You're good enough to be on that show," Misty continues, "but I know you'd never want to be on television. You're too low-key to have a television personality."

I run out of quarters. There are more in my pencil case in Nasreen's room, but my pocket is empty. "No! I will be on the show," I say.

The line goes dead, the money-hungry payphone and robotic operator cutting me off. The call had been irritating me, but I still wanted to impress my friend and tell her a little bit about what I'm up to in the city. But even when I'm in Miami, Misty and Tamara both have a way of cutting me off and rambling about themselves. Being on the phone just highlights this habit of theirs. Anger sizzles inside me. I thought we were close since I've known them since elementary school. When I'm at home, I call them every night, and we share many classes together. Being far away from them makes me doubt my friendship with them. Perhaps they're really not my friends and they have a low opinion of me. Here I am dabbling in the cool and the bad, and they don't think I'm capable of such things.

Chapter Sixteen

I'm determined to keep out of Wahib and Tahir's reach.
The only way I'm willing to touch them is if I'm exchanging
money to purchase the tape. *NYC Dance Off* is the answer to
my prayers, I'm sure of it. I'll be competing with other young
women, but I know I can dance. Even if I don't win anything, I
have to try. It's better than waiting for something to happen,
because Nasreen and I exhausted all of our other
moneymaking possibilities. The only thing left to do would be
criminal, and I'm not willing to go there, although I packed
some pantyhose in my suitcase that would be perfect for a
bank robbery.

My irritation and that nagging feeling about my friends
disrespecting me fizzle away. I can always deal with Tamara
and Misty when I'm back in Miami, maybe smooth things out
and really sit down and talk to them, gushing about what I've
been through. But what if they cut me off and still don't
believe me even when we're face-to-face? No, we're friends.
I'll get them to listen to me.

I can't think about them right now. I need to rehearse
for the show, but where? The only thing I can practice in the
basement apartment is singing since *NYC Dance Off* accepts
both singers and dancers. I haven't been in glee club since
middle school, and I took Chorus I as a freshman, but I
couldn't take Chorus II this past year because that meant

forfeiting Honors Geometry, which I wasn't willing to do, so I'm not comfortable with singing. I still want to try anyway. Nasreen is very much against the idea of me singing.

I croon Journey's "Don't Stop Believin'" in Nasreen's room.

"No, no, no," Nasreen says, covering her ears.

I switch to Elton John's "Sad Songs."

"Stop torturing me! My ears are going to bleed."

Nasreen can be mean. My singing isn't that bad. I never got to sing solo in glee club or chorus, but I was always singing in the background. I haven't stretched my singing voice. Okay, I'll admit I dance better than I sing.

I need to practice dancing. If I were to dance in Nasreen's room, I'd knock everything off her desk and bruise my arms and legs against the bunk bed. When I dance, I put everything into it. Not only am I a soccer player and aerobics fanatic, but I dance while I wait for my mom to pick me up from school. She runs errands before coming, so I have some time to kill on practice and nonpractice days. My friends and I do the cabbage patch, running man, and all the other popular dances from TV. *Can I have some fries with that shake?* I've heard. *Gimme some of that.* Even in my tomboy clothes, I get those remarks. I blush all the way to my hairline, but I continue dancing. I know I'm the best dancer out of all my friends. I'm fluid and don't run out of breath.

"You know, I've never seen you dance," Nasreen says.

"You're in for a treat," I brag.

"Then let's find a place for you to practice."

We go out to search for an area where I can practice my dance moves. Thankfully, there are no subway rides since we're looking for an open space nearby. I'm not tired of taking trains yet, but I'm subwayed out for today. Nasreen takes me to the playground, where we see Omar's dark head bent down as he huddles with his friends, his two demon whorls in full view. Nasreen stops and lingers by the fence. She clears her throat.

Omar looks up, grinning at us. Amazing. He's doing something wrong but has no misgivings. If I were gambling, I'd be worried and guilty. He walks away from his friends to meet us by the fence. The mesh separates us. Through the metal striations, I glance down at his tawny skin and smug expression.

"Having fun?" Nasreen asks.

"Yes," Omar says. "Going out again? You and Asma seem to be out a lot. I hope you're not doing anything Baba wouldn't be happy with."

"Of course not," I say in a fake, sweet voice.

"We also hope you're keeping your nose out of trouble," Nasreen says.

"I always do."

I laugh and hurry to cover my mouth. Omar narrows his eyes.

"Have fun at this little casino of yours... I mean playground," I say.

Omar's jaw drops. In spontaneous, perfect choreography, Nasreen and I both turn around at the same time, swaying our hips as we cross the street.

"I think torturing him a little bit will be fun," I say.

"That's a lot coming from you," Nasreen says. "I thought you didn't have a mean bone in your body."

"You must be rubbing off on me..."

***

We walk a few blocks to a grassy square. There's a small park, an ice cream truck, and people going about their business. Yards away from us there are some break dancers. They're fun to watch as they spin on their heads, do splits, and jump around. They leave a few minutes later, taking their boom box and cardboard mat with them. Inside the park, kids are swinging, sliding, and getting sprayed by a large sprinkler. Behind them there's a basketball court, which is in use. I'd rather not go in there, and I suppose it's not a big deal if I dance on the sidewalk leading up to the park. It's not terribly crowded. I have to practice somewhere. "We forgot to bring music," I say.

"Don't worry," Nasreen says. "My Walkman has exterior sound."

What a relief. Mine doesn't do that, and it only works with headphones. Nasreen has a giant cup of soda she was sipping from; she took the lid off minutes ago so she could suck on the ice. She puts it down on the ground so she can take her Walkman out of her purse, pull out the headphones, and then tune the radio. I hear country, elevator tunes, and oldies before she hits the pop station. Janet Jackson's "Pleasure Principle" segues into Samantha Fox's "Touch Me."

"Don't change it," I say. I love that song. I dance languidly with the slow beginning. Once the chorus begins and the guitars rev up, my body follows the tune. I spin around, shoot an arm up, and then do a split.

A young woman stops and bops her head. My hair whirls around me, and in between the strands I see two men in business suits and a group of teenagers. Quarters and dimes fly, followed by a splash. I slow down my dancing, doing some knee highs towards the end of the song, and I see where the noise is coming from. People are throwing coins into Nasreen's cup of soda, where a few slivers of melting ice remain. Nasreen's eyes widen. I'm also seeing dollar bills.

I dance to Taylor Dayne's "Don't Rush Me," followed by my favorite song... Madonna's "Into the Groove." I snap my fingers, moving my body from side to side. People come and go, throwing money into Nasreen's cup. Nasreen is the DJ, navigating between songs, changing stations once commercials begin. The only problem is that radio stations seem to synchronize their commercials. They all play them at the same time. I use that as rest time, but that's when people wander away before a new crowd comes in. At the most ten people surround me.

"No more," I say after five songs. I'm beat, and I think that was enough practice. I have a Taylor Dayne cassette in my luggage, so if I have to dance to my own music I'll bring that with me to the audition. Nasreen hands me some napkins from her purse, the ones she picked up from the fast food joint where she got her soda. The crowd dissipates, but not before several people tell me how fantastic I am.

"Baby, you're a pro."

"Do you do bachelor parties?"

I'm not ready for this attention. I shake my head bashfully at the sleazebag who asks me the last question. Nasreen swipes down, gets her cup, and pulls me along farther into the park. We find a bench by a basketball court. Men and boys are shirtless or wearing tops drenched in sweat. Normally I'd ogle, but Nasreen needs help counting the money.

The day is over with, and I no longer care about my clothes, which are just as drenched with sweat as the basketball players'. I pull down my shirt and use the bottom as a holder for the money. I take Nasreen's cup and turn it over. The ice is long gone, and all that's left is tepid water, which pours through the cotton of my shirt and onto my lap. I look at all the pennies, nickels, dimes, and a few quarters. Nasreen makes four piles in my lap. I count the pennies and nickels while she counts the rest. "Three dollars and twenty-three cents," she says.

"That's all?" I say.

"I thought we made more than that, but that's pretty good for a half hour of dancing. Maybe if you dance all day long—"

"No way." I shake my head. "I can't dance like that for hours. I'm in shape, but that would kill me. I know what you're thinking. If we can make three dollars in half an hour and if I dance for a day maybe we can make up for what we're missing to buy the tape from the perv brothers. But if I'm as good as you think, I can make even more in a shorter amount of time from *NYC Dance Off*."

"You're right. I was watching it the other day, and a girl won three hundred dollars on her first day of dancing. That was from their applause meter. I'm sure you'll get lots of applause."

"Thanks, Nasreen."

"You'll win some money this week when you make it on the show," she says.

"We have a lot to prepare for," I say. "We need to figure out what I'll wear."

"Let's go home. We both need a shower badly."

I walk with a bounce to my step. It isn't until we're a block from home that my ankle is bothering me again. There's a twinge radiating in the middle of the bone. The pain lessens until it's a minor throb. That's what I get for walking into stores with strange men who make me want to run from them and then dancing my ass off on a public street. But our situation calls for sacrifices. We will get that tape someway, somehow.

Chapter Seventeen

"Can't a girl take a shit in peace?" Nasreen shrieks when someone pounds on the door of the restaurant's bathroom.

My hair is crimped, so it zigzags from my scalp in all directions. Auntie blew on me this morning, thinking Nasreen and I dolled ourselves up to tour the city, but in reality we're going to auditions for *NYC Dance Off*. I left the basement apartment with my hair like this, but now we're in the bathroom of a Dunkin' Donuts to complete the transformation. I take off my tights and t-shirt and put on a zebra-patterned miniskirt and a pink off-the-shoulder top. Nasreen is doing my makeup. "Close your eyes," she says.

There's more pounding, but then the person ceases. We're trying to be fast, but it takes time to be a knockout. I like what I see in the mirror. Nasreen does my eyes in black, purple, and turquoise. She paints my lips in glorious fuchsia. Two thick swipes of blush display cheekbones I didn't know I had. I'm also wearing Lee Press-On Nails, my red talons transforming my hands into woman hands, not the little-girl hands of short nails and pink polish I'm used to.

"Wow," Nasreen says.

"I look..."

"Gorgeous and hot."

"Yeah," I agree.

"And look at your legs. They look awesome."

"Thanks. We soccer players do have great legs."

"We need to get to the studio," Nasreen says. "Let's avoid any lines."

It's a good thing I'm wearing LA Gear sneakers. They're comfortable for dancing, good for walking the streets, and they're fashionable with my outfit. The pink in the sneakers matches the pink of my top. Men turn towards me and whistle. Some of the guys look cute, but where are the John Stamoses in this world? They can't just be trapped inside TV tubes or chanced upon briefly in airplanes. The only men I've really talked to during my stay here were relatives and the creepy duo, Tahir and Wahib. I might as well forget about my fantasy of having a summer fling. This business of finding a replacement tape consumes me.

We reach Rockefeller Plaza, and the two of us study the address I wrote down yesterday. "That has to be it," Nasreen says, pointing to a line of people standing behind pedestrian barriers.

"That line is so long!" I say. This is worse than the cafeteria line at school. Sometimes I only have ten minutes to scarf down my food because I'm standing in line most of the time. But this is something else. We might be here all day.

"Maybe it'll move fast. Come on."

We join the line. In front of me are people who are much older than I am: men with stubble and women with lined faces. I hear one lady tell another she's twenty-nine. That's almost ancient. What's she even doing here when this show is for the young? But even though they're old, they're dressed cool, with zippers, buttons, and spangles all over their clothes.

Some skinny Prince-wannabe with a moustache and Jheri curls comes to us and asks me to pin a number on my shirt. He hands me a piece of paper with #191 written in marker, which I pin below my shoulder. Nasreen shakes her head and tells the guy she's there to support me. He moves along. "We're going to be here forever!" I whine again.

We move a few feet forward, so it isn't that bad. At least I'm making progress with the line. People are joining the line behind me. Hairspray, perfume, cologne, scrambled eggs, butter, and bad body odor mingle together in the sizzling air. Trickles of sweat begin at my hairline and make their way down the sides of my face. My makeup artist, Nasreen, blots my face with a napkin. "You're going to knock them dead," she says.

"Thanks for the support," I say.

"Really, no one's going to dance better than you. And look at the other girls with all that paint shellacked on their faces, too-tight clothes, and wrinkles. You're the prettiest young thing here."

"Pretty young thing," someone behind me sings.

I turn around to look into a pair of eyes that hit me like a laser beam. Luscious, dark hair sprouts from the top of his head. He's turned slightly away from me, and I see a braid trickle from the nape of his neck. Some of my friends make fun of guys with rattails, but I think they're hot. This guy is smoking. Black jeans, black tank top, studded belt... and the more I look at him, he looks like John Stamos. He morphs into the guy I met in the airplane. Tall, dark, and handsome.

"Abe?" I say.

"Asma?" he says.

"Oh my God," we say together, shocked at seeing each other again. I thought seeing him was a one-time thing, that we'd both be swallowed by the city and our respective families.

"What are you doing here?" I ask.

"I love to dance, so I thought why not audition since I'm in town."

"Me too!" I smile so hard that I hope my eye makeup isn't falling apart. I already feel specks of powder crumple onto my cheeks. Nasreen blots them away. That's what I get for using cheap makeup with the low funds I have.

After Nasreen fixes my makeup, she glares at Abe. One thing I've noticed about her is how distrustful she is of everyone. I'm more open to people. I'll say hi to a stranger. I'll give coins to the homeless. Nasreen is the opposite and shuts herself off from everyone. I smile at Abe, my brief companion from the airplane before some big guy ruined things by asking him to move. John Candy could've been nice and switched seats with Abe; I've switched seats for the elderly, newlyweds, and other people who belong together, and it had to be obvious Abe and I were together, even though we were strangers.

Nasreen pulls me by the elbow when we're holding up the line. We join the people in front of us, and Abe follows, his cologne, Drakkar Noir, drifting to my nostrils. It's a crisp, clean, sexy smell.

"I'm getting something to drink," Nasreen says. "I'll be right back."

Nasreen walks around the barrier and crosses the street to where a pretzel vendor is. This is excellent, because now I have some alone time with Abe. He's grinning at me.

"What a coincidence," he says. "I tried finding you at the airport when we arrived, but I didn't spot you. Plus my aunt was waiting for me."

"And my uncle was waiting for me."

"Your name is familiar. I have a grandmother named Asma."

"I'm Persian," I explain.

"I'm Syrian," he says.

He's around my age, he lives not too far from me in Miami, we're both in New York at the same time, and we're both Middle Eastern. I can't ignore this information. My summer fling might be right in front of me, but I don't have much time to chitchat. I find out that Abe is staying in

Greenwich Village, he loves to dance but break dancing is his specialty, and in the future he wants to get a basketball scholarship and later go to medical school... and he loves Madonna.

A car drives by blasting "True Blue," and I feel my body move with it. "You like Madonna?" Abe asks.

"I adore her," I say. "I wish I could go to her Madison Square Garden concert."

"I'll be going with my aunt and uncle."

"No way!"

"Yes." He nods. "Isn't there a way for you to go?"

"I don't think so. So what's your favorite song of hers?"

We start talking about music, but then Nasreen has to come back to ruin things. "This guy still bothering you?" she asks.

"No, no, he's not bothering me. He never was!"

Abe smiles at Nasreen, but he can't win her over. She glowers, looking like Sam the Eagle from *The Muppets*.

In no time, I'm in front of the line. Outdoors meets indoors. The humidity wears off, it gets cooler, drier, and I'm under air-conditioning vents. Someone ushers me inside a studio. "Oh my God, oh my God, oh my..." I stammer.

"Calm down!" Nasreen says. "Go in there and knock them dead."

"You'll do great," Abe says.

I turn around. "Thank you." I barely know him and he's already cheering for me.

"Next!" someone yells.

"There's no time to flirt," Nasreen whispers. "Get in there."

I walk on unsteady feet. I'm so glad I'm wearing sneakers. My ankle starts to throb again. Oh no!

I'm facing two guys and a woman who are behind a table and sitting on folded chairs. This is it, this is audition time, and I need to give it my all. The lights are bright, but not as bright as I thought they would be for TV. This is just an audition, not the real thing, although there is a cameraman honing in on me. His big lens is like a gigantic evil eye, a Cyclops eye. Auntie's evil-eye beads come to mind.

"How old are you?" the woman with thick, veiny fingers and harlequin glasses asks. My eyes fixate on her many rings and huge, triangular earrings. She isn't old with her unlined face, but she dresses old. She even has old-lady hair: blonde, nearly white, and short.

"You look a bit young," a middle-aged man with salt-and-pepper hair says.

"Um, I'm eighteen," I lie.

"Yeah, right," another guy says. "We can't use this footage, no way."

Music starts playing, which I didn't expect since the trio didn't seem to be done interviewing me. It's a dance beat without lyrics.

"I didn't say to start!" the woman shouts. "Cut the music! We're not done talking!"

This is my chance. I need to impress them so the inquisition about my age can end. My body moves instinctively in the large, high-ceilinged, brightly lit room. The music echoes across the walls, pounding me with its bass. I dance the same way I did in the park, with abandon. There's half a can of hairspray in my crimped hair, but the strands become limp with motion. In between my flying hair I see the blurred faces of the casting people, the cameraman, people who had been standing in the back coming closer... to see me. The pain in my ankle fades away, because this is my moment to shine.

When the music stops I hear praise, varying from crude to fancy.

"Nice ass on that girl."

"She's as light and graceful as a ballerina."

I hear all sorts of things from the gathering crowd.

People carrying sound equipment, women in curlers who are being made up, and buff men wearing tight shirts and tank tops are gaping. I break out into a smile, my face straining against my overwhelming happiness, but then my smile dies when I hear her voice.

The old but young lady, whom someone calls Faye, asks again, "But how old is she?"

"That was fantastic," the two men simultaneously say.

"Do you have a parent or guardian with you?" Faye asks.

"No," I say, shrugging my shoulders and frowning. I conjure Nasreen's mean face that she's always giving people. "I'm old enough."

"I'm afraid Faye's right," the older guy says. "You look quite young, the youngest person we've seen so far. We'll need a parent to sign a paper unless you have ID on you."

"I was so excited about coming here that I left it at home," I explain. "We can always take care of technicalities later."

"That's a shame. You're extremely talented, and I'd love to have you on the show."

"Me too," the other man echoes.

"What is your name?" Faye asks.

"I go by Hot Pink."

"Cool name," someone in the back says.

"Great stage name," another voice pipes up.

"You go by," Faye snorts, her rings clacking together as she gesticulates. "Anyone serious would reveal her real name first before handing us a pet name. You're not all that special to be a one- or two-name wonder. You're no Madonna or Boy George. Have a good day. I'm not entertaining any youngsters. I hope the next candidate has stopped teething and isn't wearing a training bra. *Next!*"

A pretty young thing in a turquoise mini ushers me out through a different door than the one I entered from. Another pretty young thing with humongous shoulder pads gives me a sympathetic smile. But I wanted to be a P.Y.T. strutting in front of a camera for money to buy a Kulthum tape, for Madonna tickets. Why is "P.Y.T." even stuck in my head? I don't talk like that. Now I remember that Abe called me that minutes ago. I hope I get to chat with him after his audition so he can commiserate with me; I'm so embarrassed and need to talk about my dashed hopes with someone.

I'll probably have a chance to talk with him. I linger by the door and see that Abe is next for his audition. The trio grills him with some questions, and a dance beat ensues.

"Stop!" Faye says. "I didn't say to start! Who the hell is cuing the music?"

The music starts prematurely, just like it had with me, and I'm glad it did. Abe is amazing.

My eyes are transfixed to his muscular body as he break-dances. First, he does footwork before going into spins. He looks like a helicopter, spinning on his feet, his back, and finally his head. When dealing with strangers you never know what you're dealing with. Standing next to Abe outside, with him all composed and still, I never imagined his body could do these moves. My heart swells with happiness for him. Even though I'm sad about my audition, at least others can make it, and I want the best for him.

"Hey, hey," a man calls out. "Move it along."

A security guard points the way out, and I pry myself away from Abe's mesmerizing dance moves. The spell is broken once I'm away from him, because sadness washes over me.

"Watch where you're going," a woman brays when I bump into her.

"Go over there," another man in a security uniform snaps. "Exit's that way."

Where's Nasreen? She was with me up to the point I stood in front of the casting people. Great, I can't find her. I meet one beige wall after another. I see water fountains, people bustling around, and sequins. Someone in wardrobe wheels clothes past me. To think that I could be wearing some of those clothes!

The futility of everything hits me. I was riding too many hopes on this show when I'm a minor. My parents aren't here to sign any forms. Even if they were, they wouldn't go for the idea of me being on TV when they think TV is for loose American girls. A good girl like me doesn't belong on TV. They tolerate me on the soccer field, with my short shorts and loose shirts, but that brings trophies home and puts my name in the paper, and it'll look good on college applications. Soccer is okay, but dancing is not. To them, being on TV is meaningless, even trashy. This also confirms the beliefs of my friends. Tamara and Misty see me as a goody-goody, someone who could never be cool and glamorous. I belong on the soccer field, dressed in boyish gear, or in the library with my nose in a book.

The crimped hair and makeup was to disguise myself in case I ended up on TV. All for nothing. I go into a restroom. When I take a paper towel to my face, indigo, violet, and fuchsia streaks mottle it; I need two more paper towels to get all the cosmetics off. The rainbow is gone, and all that's left is my bare skin. I was aggressive wiping away my makeup, and one of my nails is askew. I go ahead and rip off the flimsy, fake nails. I'm back to my stubby nails. The big, crimped hair and sexy clothes are the only un-Asma-like things left, but my face looks like me. Unglamorous me. That's how I leave the bathroom, looking for the exit, which is getting harder to find.

"Hey, beautiful," someone calls out.

I'm not in the mood for any pervy men. Thinking about the men at the park yesterday and the men just now, I realize my parents are right. They're predators, and I don't need their attention. And how can I be beautiful without any makeup and with fried, crispy hair?

"Hey, wait up!"

I spin around to confront the person. "I'm not in the mood! Go f—"

"I didn't want to leave without saying good-bye."

"Oh, it's you."

Chapter Eighteen

Uncle Jesse is here. This isn't one of my uncle-uncles, all serious, dressed in seventies polyester, smelling like mothballs, and with a handlebar moustache. This is Abe, the John Stamos look-alike, who walked out of my daydreams.

"Oh, I'm sorry," I apologize. "I thought you were someone else."

I look through my purse and take out a banana clip to hold back my hair. I'm never crimping my hair again. I miss my straight strands, because I know I'm a mess right now.

"I didn't mean to be rude. I really thought you were someone else."

"I'm jealous," he says.

"Of who?" I ask.

"Whoever it is you were waiting for."

"I'm in a rush. I'm looking for my cousin."

"The girl with spiky hair?" Abe asks.

"Yeah."

"I just saw her. She's looking for you too, but security wouldn't let her search the other wing of the building. Let me take you to her."

"Thank you."

My cheeks become heated. His smile is wry, one side of his face pulling all the way up while the other side does so halfway. He has straight, white teeth. This is a sexy, naturally lopsided smile... not what Tahir was trying to attempt with me not too long ago.

"I thought you were pretty before, but you look even better without all that junk on your face," Abe says. "How old are you? And I mean your real age."

"Sixteen," I admit, figuring he saw my downfall during auditions if he's asking about age. "What about you?"

"Sixteen. That Faye woman asked me to leave. There's no playing around her."

Sixteen? He looks eighteen. Hmmm, I never thought too much about boys my age before. I usually ignore the boys in my class and admire the upperclassmen. Every woman I know is with an older man. My dad is five years older than my mom, and Uncle is eight years older than Auntie... and I've always daydreamed about older men on the small and silver screen. When I met Abe I thought he was a high school senior or in college already. It must be his confident strut and sexiness that make him seem older.

"Your break dancing is fantastic," I say. "I seriously don't know anyone in Miami who can dance like that."

"I like to practice after school while I'm waiting for my mom to pick me up," he says.

"That's when I practice too! I dance with my friends while waiting for my ride."

We walk towards the atrium of the building, where there are stairs overlooking the lobby. I peer down and see Nasreen right away. Her spikes tower over the bangs of all the women around her. "Nasreen," I say over the din. "Nasreen!" I get her attention and she looks up. Her raccoon eyes scare me from this height. It's like looking at two pools of oil.

"What are you doing there?" she asks. "Get your ass down here."

"Come up here," I yell back. I don't want to lose her again.

"No! I'm afraid of heights."

She wouldn't want to be at the balcony-like overhang above the lobby. "All right, I'll be right there," I say.

The atrium's stairs have heavy traffic. Abe grabs me by the hand to steer me towards the one closest to us. My hand. I can't even remember the last time I held a guy's hand. It must have been in kindergarten when we had to walk in two straight lines to and from the classroom. To the side of the stairs there are windows giving me a glimpse of the outdoors. I get that same buzz I feel every time I look at busy New York streets: people are leaving work, coming back from it, sitting at outdoor restaurants, drinking coffee, shopping, singing on the streets, playing violin for change. This area is far busier than Uncle's neighborhood. The excitement grips my heart, and I stand still, even though I feel Abe's gentle pull down the stairs as people walk around us.

"What is it?" he asks.

"Nothing," I say, feeling the city while I'm indoors. "Let's go."

We walk down. Abe is holding the railing while I walk by his side. Halfway down there's a twinge in my ankle. The pain I thought was gone is back. It begins at the bony knob of my ankle and shoots up my leg. I'm only a few steps away from the lobby when I can't take the weight pressed down on my foot. I start to tumble, but Abe grips me hard.

He gets in front of me, holding me. He eases me down the steps, my chest against his, and once we're off the steps he continues to hold me. I look into his eyes. This is probably the last time I'll see him. We're two random strangers. The same electricity I feel from looking at the city radiates from his hands and through my body. I believe he's concerned about my welfare, which is why he's not letting go of me. That small tumble, that second of tripping down the stairs, turns into something else. When his face gets closer to mine, I don't flinch or think anything's strange. He kisses me on the lips. This is nothing like the Dorito-laden kiss of last year with unromantic Brad. I close my eyes, hold him for a moment, and then we break away. People surround us, but I don't see or hear them.

"Can I have your number?" he asks.

Talk! His sweet lips have stunned me speechless. "I don't think that's a good idea," I manage to say, predicting Uncle's reaction to a strange boy calling me. "Hold on." I find a piece of paper in my purse and jot down the number of the payphone. Good thing I have a great memory for numbers and that I had watched Nasreen write the number for Wahib. But the thing is, if Abe ever calls, I'm going to have to rush out whenever the phone rings. He finds a wrinkled business card in his wallet and writes down both his New York and Miami numbers on it for me.

"Who's this guy again?" Nasreen asks. I jump at the sound of her voice. I thought she was farther away, lost in the crowd, but she snuck up on us. And she's so rude!

"This is Abe," I say. "Remember, the guy I told you about who I met on the plane."

"I don't remember you telling me about him." Nasreen puffs her chest as if she's challenging him. I look at her, pleading with my eyes that she doesn't do anything embarrassing to drive him away. "So you got in the show?" she asks.

"Too young," I say, shaking my head.

"Me too," Abe says.

"Well, we gotta go. Nice meeting you, Abe." Her voice is gentler after hearing about my failure. She sounds resigned, and so am I. I didn't get the gig.

While I walk away, I turn around and catch Abe staring at me. I wish I could stay to talk to him some more, but we must get back home to plan things out. We're trying so hard, and I won't give up now. How do we get a replacement tape now that *NYC Dance Off* is a no-go?

***

The rest of the day is all ours. I had imagined I would spend the day in makeup and wardrobe—doing all that showbiz stuff I've fantasized about—but I'm back in the basement. The only reminder of the morning is my crimped hair and tingling lips. It's as if my lips have their own memory separate from my brain.

Nasreen steps out to develop the film of her brother's gambling notebook. Omar is out playing and gambling. I'm alone with Auntie. She's in the kitchen making baklava and spreading the layers of phyllo pastry, butter, and ground walnut on top of each other. I would like to help, but I'm more of a cook than a baker, and I don't have a light touch with phyllo since I've ripped it before. I want to broach the subject of Nasreen's desire to leave New York. If I can't replace the Umm tape, I can at least help Nasreen with this other goal of hers.

"I think it's interesting that you have a degree in chemistry," I say.

"I went to the University of Tehran," she says. "I made so many friends and had wonderful professors. I still keep in touch with many of them."

"Everyone says college life is fun."

"Yes, it is. I felt homesick, but my new friends made me feel comfortable."

"You were homesick?" I ask.

"Yes." She nods. "My family lived in Kashmar, not Tehran."

So she left home to go to college. Anger at this hypocrisy burns down my throat and chest. I control my feelings, because I'm sure Auntie has her reasons. "So why can't Nasreen leave home for college?"

"This isn't Iran. It's dangerous here. The city has many good colleges, and there's no reason for Nasreen to go into a strange environment. But you know what? One thing may change my mind."

"What's that?" I ask. I lean forward, almost tipping my stool over.

"If I see a sign." Auntie stops spreading walnut across the pastry and looks to the ceiling, as if looking to heaven. "If Allah sends me a sign that Nasreen is meant to leave New York, I will talk my husband into it and she will go where she so desires."

"A sign? What kind of sign?"

"It all depends," Auntie says. "There are signs all around us."

This is all cryptic and over my head. Middle Eastern people have all sorts of superstitions, and I've only learned a few of them dealing with my elders. There are so many superstitions and signs I have yet to discover. Maybe a sign will come to Auntie that she should let Nasreen go to the city and college of her choice.

I go to Nasreen's room and climb onto my bed. Since I'm alone, I go ahead and pull back the curtains to watch people come and go, talk into the payphone, and dribble basketballs. I get some looks since I'm on ground level staring up at people, so I pry my eyes away and work on my scrapbook.

Leaving Abe's number in my wallet, I pull out the #191 sign from my audition and paste it into my scrapbook. It's a sign of failure, but at least I had the guts to put myself out there. I thought it would be so easy to get in by looking good and dancing like a maniac, but I was wrong. Dreams may not always pan out, but life wouldn't be worth living if I didn't pursue them.

Once I paste the number, there's an empty page facing me that I want to fill. I step down, grab a pile of magazines Nasreen plans to throw out, and bring them to my bed. I look through them and cut out a picture of a model with shapely shoulders, a moth, a beaded necklace, and a few other items that remind me of superstitions I've heard come out of

Auntie's mouth.

I'm getting an idea. It's huge and crazy, but maybe I can create the sign that will unlock Nasreen from this basement that she's tired of. I messed up with the tape and *NYC Dance Off*, but I can't be a complete failure. I must get something right on this trip. I'll do this for my cousin so she can have the life she wants.

Chapter Nineteen

"Where is my Umm Kulthum tape?" Uncle yells. He looks from box to box. Heavy rain pounds against the sidewalk, but the boisterous tinkling of water doesn't drown out his anger and confusion. It's only been a week since we've destroyed the tape, yet it feels like much longer with my incessant panic and all the running around town I've done. We could only hold him off for so long.

"Calm down!" Auntie says. "It must be here somewhere."

"But where?" Uncle wonders. The shelves have no backing. He tries to pull the entertainment system from the wall to see if the tape fell behind it. His stringy muscles bulge out of his arms, but the shelves are too heavy.

"Don't strain yourself."

"I can't move this," he says. "I would have to remove the TV, books, magazines, music... everything. I've lost a few tapes, and they're all behind there. I never bothered to look, but now I want to because I haven't heard Kulthum in a while."

"You've been working hard all day. Wait until the weekend when Nasreen and Asma can help you pull it all out and you can check if the tape is there."

"And I'll help too," Omar says, sticking his head out of the curtains. His smile is smug, as always. When he sees

Nasreen and me on the couch, he narrows his eyes. He didn't like our innuendo the other day at the fence of his playground. Well, we have more in store for him since Nasreen developed the photos.

"Let's get ready for bed," Nasreen says. That's code for "let's get ready for a night in the closet."

We take turns in the bathroom. I hear beeping and other electronic noises as Omar plays games behind his curtains, but then they cease. His parents think he's up early during summer vacation because he has a lot of energy to burn. Yeah, that and he has his gambling ring at the corner playground. As early as ten in the morning his friends knock on the door to see if he's up and ready.

Uncle checks the locks of the front door before he retires. That's our cue to go into the closet to watch TV. Nasreen enters the closet first.

"I'll be right there," I tell her. Opening a drawer, I pull out my cosmetics. I dab cream on my face and balm on my lips. Then I proceed to put lotion on my arms. The only light that's on is the desk light, which is dim, but I'm still able to study myself in the mirror. I brush my hair and pout, imagining I'm getting ready to see Abe. I have his number and he has the number of the payphone, but he hasn't called yet. I doubt I'll ever see him again. I can mark him off as a new experience I had during my stay in the Big Apple. His was the first kiss I experienced—I'm not counting my time with Brad and his Dorito breath. Abe was the real deal.

My daydreaming comes to a halt when Nasreen calls for me. "Asma, come in here right now," she whispers.

"What is it?"

"Get in," she urges in a louder tone.

I rush into the closet, plopping down next to her. Holy crap.

NYC Dance Off is playing. It plays twice a day—in the afternoon and it re-airs at night. I didn't bother watching it earlier today since I was depressed about my unsuccessful audition. I'm over it now, but it still stings. Now that I'm watching it, I see that I did make it into the show.

"This line is unbelievable," a hostess with lilac eye shadow and purple lips announces. "These people are all auditioning for the show, and some of them were here as early as five this morning, camping outside the building..."

In the corner of the screen, I see a familiar rattail. It's the back of Abe's head. Then I come into view. There's my crimped hair and outlandish, hip clothes.

"I didn't see a camera in front of me," I whisper.

"You've been on for the past few minutes, first walking down the stairs, then tripping, and then Abe was holding you in the lobby," Nasreen says.

Abe leans toward me for the kiss. It's a melding of my crimped hair and his bushy bangs before we part.

"Oh no," I gasp.

"Shit," Nasreen blasts. She lowers her voice and says, "I didn't know you two kissed. What's wrong with you? You're not supposed to kiss strangers. And haven't you heard of AIDS?"

"You can't get AIDS from kissing," I reply. "I can't believe I'm on camera. Do you think I look recognizable?"

"Kind of," Nasreen says. "It looks like you took off your makeup, which you shouldn't have, but the clothes and hair alter your looks."

"They do," I agree. The thing is, because I recognize myself, I assume other people will. "But my parents don't watch this show. My brothers don't even like this sort of music. Anyway, I'm in the background. It's not like they zoomed in on us."

"Yeah, let's think positive. If I hadn't been with you, I might not know it's you on the screen since you left here in different clothes."

The camera pulls away from the hostess and focuses on

the actual show, where an emcee is announcing a band, then the camera pans to the dancers, to a world I was almost a part of. They look so happy and free, smiling, spinning, and pumping their arms in the air. Again, I feel bad that I'm not in this crowd. I have my nose pressed against the window. I want to be on the other side, having fun and being hip.

"What a bummer," I say. "And we still have to think of a fast way to get money for the replacement tape."

"With the pictures I developed, I think we can get our money back from Omar and then some," Nasreen says. "I just have to figure out a way to approach him since he's such a sneaky bastard."

"I'll cross my fingers that everything pulls through," I say. "With this tape, with Omar, and even with you leaving New York."

"Dream on, Pollyanna," Nasreen huffs. She changes the channel, switching from the bouncy youth of *NYC Dance Off* to *David Letterman*. It's cool that a guy old enough to be our dad is so funny, but it's not cool that Nasreen is negative and thinks I'm a Pollyanna. I believe in happy endings, as hard as they are to come by.

***

Voices disrupt my sleep. Every time I startle awake I hear a different sound. A woman cries, a dog barks, a man is yelling and asks for his money back, a woman requests a collect call. Then the phone rings. I pry my lids open and look at the clock. It's nine thirty. It rings and rings, shrill in my ear. It's a few feet from the window, but it might as well be in the room with me. When it rings again, it's a quarter past ten. I was up all night watching TV, hoping I could sleep until noon, but this phone is relentless.

"Nasreen!" I moan. "The payphone keeps ringing and no one's picking it up."

"It must be for us," she says. She rolls out of bed, literally. She falls to the floor, stumbles on her knees, and is on her feet reaching for her clothes.

"Oh, yeah," I say, having forgotten that Wahib, Tahir, and my one-kiss-stand all have the payphone number. I leap onto the floor and get ready. In ten minutes we're both sitting in the living room, watching Auntie boil tea so she can read leaves, something she does frequently. Auntie and Uncle usually close the curtains since anyone can peek into their basement apartment, so we don't have to worry about Auntie seeing us from the windows if we were to answer the payphone.

The phone rings again, the sound dim in the midst of the boiling water. The living room isn't directly in front of the phone like Nasreen's room is, but we hear it nonetheless. "We're going to say hi to Omar and his friends!" Nasreen says in one breath. We're out the door, not even looking back to see Auntie's reaction.

Nasreen gets to the phone first, and I'm at her side. She picks up on the sixth ring and turns the phone so the receiver is sandwiched between us. I wince, smelling the musty residue of other people's breaths. It's a mélange of all the bad odors of this world. My cousin is kind enough to turn the end farther away from our noses. "Don't talk too loud since my mom's inside," she whispers.

"Sure thing." Whether I'm outside or in the closet, I always have to keep it down.

"Hello," Nasreen says. Her voice is strained and guarded, as it usually is.

"Hello," I say all cheery, thinking of Abe.

"Ladies, it's Wahib. Can you make it to our store today? I'd like to make a deal regarding the tape."

"Is it cheaper?" Nasreen asks.

"Not exactly. But I'm ready to strike a bargain, and I believe it's something you won't be able to resist."

"We'll be there today," Nasreen says.

We go back inside, get our purses, tell Auntie we're

hitting museums, and then we head to the closest subway station. The stench of urine and the darkness hit us as we descend the stairs.

"Whether or not the tape really is in his private collection, he probably had no takers," Nasreen says, her voice echoing in the stairway. "Maybe he's back in reality and will charge us a few bucks, which I have on me. And I still have the money we borrowed from Mom."

"I think you're right," I say. "See, things are already looking up."

"Hold your horses. Remember, don't be too eager."

I can't help feeling a bit eager all the time. So many strange, exciting things have happened to me here. It's been quite a ride. I feel like my trip is winding down now that we're getting closer to the tape, which I'm sure will be in our possession soon.

Chapter Twenty

Three men carrying brown paper bags exit the store. The bags are rectangular, as always, with videos. They smile, one of them elbowing the other in the stomach. When I have an afternoon to myself to purchase tapes and videos, I smile like that too. But I have no time for enjoyment when I'm chasing this tape.

"Obviously those videos aren't one hundred dollars a pop, or else this place wouldn't be in business," I say.

"I know," Nasreen says. "How dare these two assholes try to charge us a hundred bucks just because they can smell our desperation? Let's go inside to see what they're charging today."

"Ladies!" Wahib brays when we come in, the door tinkling as it opens. The curtains from the backroom swish open as he walks into the main area of the store. "Come in, come in."

The quiet brother, Tahir, sits on a stool by the cash register as usual. He smiles at us, the space between his front teeth pitch-black, or maybe that's nicotine or decay.

"So you'd like to sell us the tape?" Nasreen asks.

"Not quite," Wahib says. "I'd like to give it to you."

I smile, but then I turn grim. Nasreen advised me to not look or sound desperate. "At no charge?" I ask.

"No, there is a charge."

"What is it?"

"Yeah, what?" Nasreen says.

"Like I said before, we'd like your, Isma's, companionship for my brother Tahir here. One meeting, one date to see how the two of you would hit it off."

For a green card. For that sleazy, disgusting brother of his. "I thought you had a new deal," I say. "Nothing has changed, and you're asking for the same thing."

"Oh, but things have changed," Wahib says. "We have something to show you."

"The tape?" Nasreen asks.

"No, something even more interesting." He turns around and aims a remote at a TV. The television's light bursts from the center until the whole screen glows. Then I see the lady from last night, the one who's all purple, and then the rattail. My jaw drops as I watch myself tripping down the stairs—I hadn't seen that in Nasreen's closet, and I look like a clumsy dork when my ankle fails me—and there's my kiss with Abe. It's surreal watching it again. My first hot, tempestuous, authentic kiss was televised for the public to see. Such a private moment ended up on tape. Knowing these two brothers, and how they seem to enjoy torturing Nasreen and me, they probably had it on rewind. Pervs. No one can see our lips actually touching. It's more like the back of Abe's head eclipsing my face, but it's obvious what we were doing.

"You have a tape of this?" I ask.

"We never miss an episode of *NYC Dance Off.* It's become our favorite show."

Tahir nods. "We love that show," he says. I don't see the both of them as dancing types, but appearances are deceiving.

"It's better than *Solid Gold* and *Soul Train,*" Wahib says.

"So you saw my friend on the show," Nasreen says. "What of it?"

"What of it?" Wahib says. "I'll tell you what. I never forget a customer. In the five years I've owned this store I've had a fantastic memory for names and faces. You're Farhad's daughter. You're not Shireen, but you're Nasreen. You came to this store two years ago with your father. You even had the same hair, same look, same everything. Your father comes here frequently for music. In fact, he came here two months ago, and I sold him a videotape of Turkish music. And I believe Isma is not your real name. That's okay. We will come to a relationship of trust so that you'll share your name with me soon. Oh, and you two look alike, so I can guess this is your sister or cousin, and not a friend."

"Okay, so you know who we are," I say. "We just want a tape, nothing else."

"But I want something, and you haven't fulfilled my request. Farhad left his business card with me. I know he's a translator living in Manhattan. I wonder what he would say if I called to tell him about how the two of you are here constantly, asking for this tape. Maybe I can even say that one of you have taken a shine to my brother here. I also have proof you've been here several times." He nods toward the ceiling. I look up to see the eye of a security camera. Great.

"So you want one meeting?" I ask.

"Yes, and you don't have to agree to anything after that."

Nasreen clears her throat. I'm feeling ill. These men are no good. They tricked us into coming here today, and they're tricking me into a date with the yucky guy at the register. Who knows, maybe by the end of this trip I'll really be married. But I can't be, since I'm only sixteen. I picture them kidnapping me to a state where I'm legal. What am I getting myself into, and all for a tape?

"Can we think things over and call you tonight?" I ask. "I have to see when I'm free. My Uncle Farhad is not a permissive man, you know."

"Sure," Wahib says. "We'll expect a call tonight. We live upstairs and we share the same phone line as the store."

"You'll hear from us tonight," Nasreen says.

I say a shaky good-bye and leave. Across the street is the school with summer sessions. Kids exit the building, and they're quite cheerful considering they're spending their summer hours at school. I would hate summer school. They're carefree as they sprint across the schoolyard, throw balls, and laugh with friends while I'm miserable thinking about how everything has snowballed out of proportion. A destroyed tape has led me to two perverted men who want me, and they have proof I was on TV when I shouldn't have been.

"Maybe we should just tell your father the truth," I say. "Yes, he'll never trust us again. Maybe he'll never want me to visit again, and I know my parents will be ashamed of me."

"Or we can press on," Nasreen says.

"How are we going to stall these guys?" I ask.

"Hold on a minute." Nasreen stops in her tracks. Waiting by a bus stop are the three guys we saw leaving the store before we arrived. They're all young, two slender and one a little pudgy. Two are brunet and one has light brown hair. They're all laughing and talking in Arabic. I don't know much Arabic, but Nasreen is still as she listens on.

"What are they saying?" I ask.

"I'm not sure, but I know Arabic dirty words when I hear them."

One of the men takes his brown paper bag and pulls the video half out. I see a woman with curly black hair, lips red and shiny like the skin of an apple, and straps of a dress lining her shoulders. No, it's lingerie.

The men laugh some more, and the one guy showing off the video slips it back into the bag.

"Did you see what I just saw?" I ask.

"Yes, but I'm not sure," Nasreen says.

"Me neither."

"If it is what I think I saw, then we'll have something on those two brothers."

"Which will cancel out what they have on us..." This fills me with excitement and hope.

"There's just one way to find out."

"How?"

"We must take it," she says.

"What do you mean?" I ask.

"We need to go over to them and take one of their bags."

"We can't steal," I say.

"Sure we can," Nasreen says. "I'll do it if you're such a wuss, but the thing is you're the athlete and the runner."

"You're right. I don't want the men to chase and overpower you. I'll take it."

"Don't worry about me," Nasreen says, squeezing my arm. "If we lose sight of each other, just go home and I'll meet you there."

I'm destroying tapes, hiding in closets, kissing strange boys, and two yucky men are blackmailing me... I might as well add mugging to the list. I'm turning into a criminal.

A bus pulls up. I watch the men through the glass and metal of the bus shelter. They stand up. One by one they get on the bus. The last guy, the one with light brown hair, is waiting to move forward, his foot up in the air to get on.

I run around the bus shelter in a counterclockwise motion, reach the man, snatch the paper bag out of his hand, and run as if I'm on the PE field.

"Hey!" he yells behind me.

He isn't as fast as I am. No one is. I'm a soccer star, scoring the most goals on my team. No one can beat me. I run one long block followed by a shorter one along quiet, residential streets that don't have lights, but I do pause at a few stop signs. I hear "bitch," "thief," and "stop that mugger," but no one is stopping me. I'm too fast, with my vision and entire being focused on winning. The words the man is saying would normally hurt my feelings, but I'm too pumped with adrenaline, as well as curiosity. I want to know what's on the tape. What are Wahib and Tahir selling behind that curtain of theirs, where they didn't want us roaming inside of when we were there last week? The police could arrest me for this, which would mean more trouble for me, but I don't think that's going to happen.

I see a police car to the right of me, with a tall, thin officer in uniform stepping out, so I turn left at a corner. No, no, nobody will catch me. I will not only find out what's on this videotape, but I'll have that Umm Kulthum tape. I'm doing too much, working too hard, to fail.

The man's voice dies down, and then I stop hearing him. I've lost him. Maybe he stopped where the police car was to report me to the officer. I need to get to a subway, fast. I've run for so long that I don't know where I am. I see small buildings, stores, and children playing. It looks similar to the neighborhood of the store, but I know I'm farther away.

I look around, thinking Nasreen may spot me. She doesn't appear, which is okay because she told me to go home if she couldn't catch up with me. I step inside a grocery store and ask the cashier where the closest subway station is. This'll be my first time alone in the subway. If someone told me days ago to travel alone on the subway, with no guidance from friends or family, I would've said no. This is the new me. I listen to the cashier tell me how many rights and lefts I need to make, and I'm out.

I take the trip by myself. In the train, when everyone looks absorbed in a magazine, newspaper, or window-gazing, I look into the paper bag without pulling the video out. I have to stifle a groan of shock... everything about the two brothers makes sense.

Chapter Twenty-One

I don't want to walk in on Auntie by myself, so I walk around the block a few times. When I pass the playground Omar isn't there, which is a blessing. I don't need him wondering what I'm doing by myself, without Nasreen. We're like each other's shadows this summer.

Every time I see someone with spiky, black hair, I walk toward the person. After a few false alarms, it's really her. "Hey!" she yells from across the street. She jaywalks to catch up with me. "I was looking for you but figured you were so far ahead of me you couldn't find me."

"Yes," I say. "I made it here alone. What an experience. I can't believe I did that!"

"I know. You're a soccer star, or so you've told me since I haven't watched you play. I know you can dance, and now I know you can mug and run. You were amazing! Good for you, for us. Let's go inside and look at the contents of that bag."

We've learned our lesson regarding Omar. He's not at home, but we're not taking any chances of him walking in on us. Nasreen sticks a chair under the doorknob, and we settle on the floor. The paper bag is in my lap, and I upturn it onto the carpet. The video tumbles out.

THESE WOMEN AREN'T WEARING YOUR JADDA'S PANTIES

NASTY, NAUGHTY MIDDLE EASTERN BABES

A LUSTFUL VIRGIN BRIDE, TOUCHED FOR THE VERY FIRST TIME

Along with thinking that whoever wrote the smutty blurb for this video was ripping off Madonna, I'm disgusted. *Jadda* means "grandmother," and the woman on the tape certainly isn't wearing big granny underwear but itty-bitty pieces of fabric. I've never seen porn before. I look at the young lady on the cover who's wearing a corset, panties, and garter belts. She has thick eyebrows, dark eyes, and curly hair... she could be a relative or family friend. It's incongruous that she's a porn star. My parents always told me that Western girls did things like this. No, they're wrong. All types of girls end up in porn.

"Whoa," Nasreen murmurs. "Arabian porn. Who would have thought this existed?" She picks up the video and looks at the lingerie-clad model and the blurb, which is in English and Arabic.

"So those two icky brothers are selling porn in the back of their store," I say.

Nasreen slides the video from the cover. "Too bad we can't watch this now," she says, shaking her head. "I'm sure my parents and Omar will go out this week to do something, and then we'll get to watch."

"I don't want to watch this!" I say. "I've never seen porn, and it's just—just—I don't know... wrong."

"Don't be a prude. I'm curious, so I'm gonna watch it with or without you." She opens her closet and puts the tape in the bottom, under a mishmash of magazines and clothes. We'll both be dead meat if our relatives find us in possession of such a thing.

"Okay, let's get to business," I say. "Obviously, they don't want everyone to know they're selling porn. It's in a backroom, and they're not advertising it in the front of the store."

"And there's another major detail," Nasreen says.

"Which is what?" I ask.

"There's a school in front of them. I read somewhere that porn stores can't be near schools. That has to be one reason they're selling porn on the down low. What they're doing is illegal!"

Once she says that golden word, *illegal*, I'm elated. Even back in Florida, sometimes my parents drive past adult stores, and none of them are near any schools because of zoning laws. "Let's get them," I say.

We discuss a plan, but then I worry that we're two young women facing two bigger men. "I want to call someone to help us," I say.

"You're right," Nasreen says. "I know some guys who'd be willing to rough these two up for us, but they're out of town for the summer."

"I know a guy... Abe."

"But you barely know him."

"I know, but he did give me his number, and he seems interested in me. I told him my family wouldn't want him calling us, so maybe I've discouraged him. I did give him the payphone number, but since we're not always home I have no idea if he's called me or not. Let's call him. Who knows? Maybe he'll want to be a part of our crazy plan to get the tape from the brothers and get back at them for all the agony they put us through."

"Okay, go call him," Nasreen says.

Auntie pulls out the vacuum, so I don't have to worry about her hearing my conversation with Abe. I step outside to use the payphone.

I call, and he picks up on the second ring. I'm tongue-tied at first but then slip easily into conversation.

"I've been trying to call the number you gave me, but there's no answering machine and some weird guy picked up and yelled at me."

"I'm sorry, but this is a payphone," I say. "I hope the guy wasn't too rude."

"No, just loud and he asked me if I'm the devil," Abe says.

"Which you're absolutely not."

He tells me he has two extra Madonna tickets since his Aunt and Uncle can't make it to Madison Square Garden next week. Can I go? Nasreen is welcome to join us. Well, isn't that sweet, considering that she wasn't very nice to him?

Even though I'm dying to go, it feels odd to receive something so huge. I've watched my parents protest large gifts, which I've also done, so that instinct kicks in. "Are you sure?" I ask. "You want me to go?"

"Of course," he says. "I don't really know too many people up here, and at the audition you mentioned you love Madonna."

"I sure do."

"So come with me."

"Okay!" I say. I don't think about asking Uncle's permission or my parents'. I'm going. I'll find a way to go. What a blessing this is, to see my idol in concert when I so badly wanted to win or buy tickets. The opportunity has come to me. I forgot to bring her tape with me, which led to all this, and now I can see her live, in the flesh in front of me. I'm breathless.

"I look forward to going with you," he says.

"I can't wait!" I say.

"My relatives aren't too keen on the music anyway, and they made other plans for that night," he says. "It was passed onto them by someone else."

Now they're being passed onto me. "Thank you for offering these tickets," I say when I'm able to breathe again. "You have no idea what it means to me. Thank you, thank you, thank you... Oh, I'm sorry to spring this on you when you've been so kind to me, but I need a favor..."

I explain what I want him to do to help us get the Kulthum tape. I worry he'll think the arrangement is too complicated, but Abe agrees to visit Wahib and Tahir's store tomorrow afternoon to assist us with our stakeout. "It's no problem," he says. "It might even be fun."

We're going to bring those brothers down. I call them next and tell them I agree to their terms and I'll be there tomorrow, around the time Abe is supposed to arrive. My voice is phony and sweet, as if I'm willing to go on a lunch date with Tahir. Wahib sounds so smooth and smug, as if he's getting his way. Tahir can take me out for lunch... in his dreams. Those two will be on the receiving end of our ambush.

***

"I'm going to need your help talking your dad into letting us go to the Madonna concert next week," I tell Nasreen when I'm back inside. I give her a description of the two phone calls and how we're going to meet the brothers tomorrow. Then I linger on the fact that Abe has Madonna tickets.

"Uh-oh," she says. "Let me think about this."

"How can we approach your dad about this?" I wonder. "And I don't want to lie either. I'm tired of hiding things with all this cloak-and-dagger stuff I've been doing this summer."

"We can tell him we scored tickets from some people who couldn't go and we're going in their place — that is the truth, right? I'll also say it's your dying wish to see Madonna in concert. I'm sure he won't fuss too much when he'll want to please you."

"Yeah, that sounds good. We're two girls who just happen to be going with a guy I just met. When I get back to Florida I want to keep in touch with Abe."

"Come on, Asma. You barely know him."

"I know, but it's what I want. The magic of a summer fling, to meet someone and instantly like him. And maybe this is more than a fling if we can see each other in Miami."

"I don't know what it is you have with him. Well, at least someone is getting her way."

I feel bad for Nasreen. The college brochures on her desk are constant reminders of her wish. I have an idea to help her, so I'm going to put it into action. But, just like the call to Wahib and Tahir, I can't do it alone.

"Do you have the pictures you took of Omar's notebook?" I ask.

"Yes."

"We need to approach him with them now," I say. "We can get our money back from him. Also, I think he can help you leave this place." Then I launch into plan-building. Two plans in one afternoon. The first to get the tape and the second to sway Nasreen's parents to let her leave home.

"Your mom wants to see a sign from the heavens telling her it's okay for you to leave, then that's what we'll give her," I continue. "Superstitions are supposed to happen naturally and by accident, but we can bring the superstitions to her."

"By faking them?" Nasreen says.

"Exactly," I murmur. "Instead of waiting for the signs, we'll make them happen."

"Umm, okay," she says. "It's kind of strange, but it might work."

Nasreen grabs the envelope of pictures from a desk drawer, and we head to the alcove. The only time we've been behind the curtains was when we snuck in when Omar was out. This time we want to be invited inside. Nasreen knocks on the wall. The sound of a clicking joystick stops, and the curtains part. I'm in front of Oz.

"What do you want?" Omar sneers, flashing angry eyes at us.

"Can we come in?" I ask.

"Okay, but just for a minute. I had to put this game on pause."

Omar sits on the sofa, and Nasreen throws the envelope on the coffee table. "The jig is up, you little twerp."

Omar picks up the envelope. His jaw drops as he fans out the pictures in his hands. "You invaded my privacy!" he says. "How dare you."

"How dare we?" I say. "You rob us blind just because we were using your dad's radio, meanwhile you're gambling."

"Hand us back our money or else I tell Mom and Dad," Nasreen says. "They'll never believe their precious little son is capable of this, but we know better. The negatives aren't in that envelope, so don't even think about doing anything with those pictures."

"Cut to the chase," Omar says. "What do you want? Just the money?"

"Yes, our money and something else," I say.

Omar wipes his face with his hands and his body slumps, his form becoming smaller on his sofa bed. The mighty prince has fallen. "What else?"

"Let's face it, Omar, you probably want the place all to yourself. You know Nasreen wants to go elsewhere for college. If she leaves, you can have her room."

"Hmmm, it would be better than this little space," Omar says, looking around the alcove.

"But you know your parents are resistant to the idea," I say. "We need your help convincing them otherwise. We're especially going to play on your mom's belief in superstitions, which will also influence your father."

"I'm listening..."

I reveal my ideas in full to Nasreen and Omar. "It's worth a try," Nasreen says.

"It's crazy," Omar says. "But I can help."

"Great." Yes, my plan to help Nasreen is a bit crazy, but it's better than doing nothing. Nasreen pouting, crying, and collecting brochures will get her nowhere. If she wants to leave New York, we have to think outside the box. I might be a quiet suburban girl from Florida, but I still have dreams to fulfill. My friends back home think that unless I'm on the soccer field I stay on the sidelines not doing anything, but they're wrong. I'm getting what I want. Sure, some things take longer to acquire than others, but I believe everything will fall into place, Pollyanna that I am.

***

For the first night since getting here, there's no closet time. We go to bed early since there's a full day ahead of us. I sleep well, unaware of any disturbances outside my window. The silence, whether I imagine it or not, almost feels like home. I think back to my quiet little street in Miami, aching for it, the first feelings of homesickness burrowing their way into my heart. Even though New York is a blast with both the good and the bad, it's too much excitement. I want my old life back, although I know this experience will change me forever. When I get back to Miami I might surprise people with crimped hair, kisses, and secrets.

We wake up early. To kill some time I play with our accessories for the stakeout. I take handcuffs out of my purse and put one cuff around my left wrist. It's tight, and I wrap the other cuff around my right wrist more loosely. I pull my hands apart a few inches, the only leeway the cuffs allow me. So this is what criminals go through. The handcuffs are toys, but they look like the real thing.

"Stop playing around with those!" Nasreen says.

"I can't help it," I say. "They're fun."

"I knew there was a kinky side to you."

Nasreen sits at her desk, looking through college brochures for the millionth time. They all look appealing. They have autumn colors of brown and green with wide lawns and majestic, old buildings. Students are using microscopes, making pottery, and doing math equations. Everyone looks interested and engaged as they leave their childhoods behind to join the adult world. These brochures

156

make me want to look for colleges soon. Nasreen has studied them so much that they're wrinkled and bent. I recognize a few of them as recent ones that arrived in the mail days ago. Nevertheless, they look worn, read endlessly by Nasreen.

"We'll get you there," I whisper.

Nasreen looks down at her collection of brochures, her eyes black pools of mascara and shadow. I wonder if she wears that much makeup to hide what's behind her eyes. Deep down I know she has a soft side. I see that every time she wants to help me, and her desires are transparent when she talks about leaving New York.

Nasreen puts her brochures in a neat pile on her desk. "You ready to go?" I ask her.

"Yes, let's get that tape."

For the first time, out of my own will and not because I'm going to a funeral, I'm wearing all black, matching Nasreen's wardrobe. It's for our mission to get the Kulthum tape.

Chapter Twenty-Two

Abe lives closer to the store than we do. I call him on the payphone and he tells me he's just about to leave. That means he should get there a little earlier than us as planned. I turn to Nasreen and cross my fingers. I know how the subway system is and we've been stuck in tunnels in delayed trains, so we decide to leave now. If we're early, we'll watch Abe from across the street.

The sky is overcast, and it drizzles on and off. Omar opts to stay inside. He looks at us talking on the phone through the kitchen window. He may be a snoop, but he doesn't know about all the things we've been through. It feels good that we can go about our business without him tattling on us. He can't say, "Baba, Nasreen and Asma are sneaking out doing something suspicious." Nasreen has the negatives and photos in a safe place, in the bowels of her closet.

We're on the subway, on another long ride to Wahib and Tahir's store, and we're hoping this will be our last time going there. When we get to Brooklyn, we sit on the steps outside the school. Sure, we're wearing black, and sunglasses are hiding our eyes since we're on a stakeout, but we fit in. We could pass as girls waiting for siblings to come out.

I see a familiar figure inside the store. "It's him!" I gasp.

"Oh, him," Nasreen says in a lackluster tone when she sees Abe. She doesn't seem to take to the idea of my summer fling. She only sees Abe as a vehicle to get what we need: the tape. Abe looks out at us, and then we lose sight of him as he goes deeper into the store. I feel scared for him, as if the two brothers are more than porn peddlers. They remind me of the witch in Hansel and Gretel. Maybe they lure men with nude women and they never come out of the store again. But that's silly, since I've seen their customers leave intact and gloating on the wings of their freshly bought porn.

I look at my watch. It's been almost ten minutes since we've seen Abe. "It's time," I say.

"Let's rock and roll," Nasreen says.

I push my sunglasses up. We march across the street and into the store. I see the trio: Wahib and Tahir are smiling at their newest customer, Abe, who has the familiar paper bag in his hands. On cue, Abe pulls the video out of the bag.

"Thanks so much, guys," he says in a loud voice. "I've been searching for porn, and this is the only store in my area that has it!"

The brothers widen their eyes, alarmed at Abe's slip.

"No, no," Tahir says.

"Be quiet!" Wahib says, pulling at Abe's arm. He tries to steer Abe to the curtained area, but it's too late.

Abe resists, shaking Wahib's hands off him and says, "I've got to go. But thanks again for selling me this porn!"

He may dance and play basketball like a pro, but he's a horrible actor.

Tahir laughs. "He's just kidding," he tells us. "This is a dance video."

"Yeah, dirty dancing," Nasreen says.

"And we're not talking about Johnny and Baby here," I say.

"Yeah!" Abe shrieks, wiggling his hips like Elvis.

"The jig is up," I pronounce, pulling a wallet from the back pocket of my black jeans. I open the wallet and flash a badge, quickly closing it. I don't want the two men to see that it's a cheap toy badge from Omar's stash of toys. Nasreen does the same with her fake badge. Then we pull out the handcuffs. Nasreen holds her pair up with menace in her eyes. She's so good at being scary. On the other hand, I twirl my cuffs on my index finger, and they drop on the floor. So much for being a suave undercover detective.

Nasreen glares at me and I pick up the cuffs. I've watched endless hours of *Cagney & Lacey* and *21 Jump Street*, and I believe I can pull this off, despite my bumbling. "You've been caught red-handed in our sting operation," I say.

"Yeah, we're undercover," Nasreen says.

"Impossible!" Tahir screeches. "You're too young."

"It's a special operation of the NYPD," I say. "We're young and unassuming enough to catch people like you in criminal acts. Also, we lied about our age. We just look like teenagers."

"But, but you were on that TV show."

"Cops don't dance? I can't have a hobby?" I'm fast with the rejoinders, even though I'm trembling on the inside. He wants to disprove me, but I won't let him. Today I'm a pretend cop going after something I want.

"You're two businessmen who like to dabble in the arena of naked ladies," Nasreen accuses.

"And you're trying to change the subject," I say.

"That's not going to work," Nasreen intones. "Boy, are you in trouble. I can't wait to book these two."

"It's going to be ugly for them when they're in custody."

"I don't think they'll last a night in the slammer."

"Whoa!" Abe says. "What's going on? Am I in trouble?"

"No, no, this is just a misunderstanding," Wahib insists. He tries again to steer Abe into the backroom, but Abe brushes his hands away. He isn't going to leave us alone with these two men. He'll protect us if need be, and he's still playing the role of the shocked, dopey customer.

"You're facing some serious charges," I say. "Across the

street from a school! You're violating, like, a dozen statutes."

"Shocking!" Nasreen erupts. "Those poor children are so close to this debauchery."

"What's going on here?" Abe yells. "I can't be here! I'm already on parole, and my officer won't be happy if I get into trouble again. I won't be happy, either!"

"No, no, there's no trouble and this is a misunderstanding," Wahib repeats.

"Hold on, hold on, surely there's been a mistake," Tahir says. "Gregory, can you please step aside so I can talk to these young women?"

Gregory is Abe's acting name for this performance. He finally allows Wahib to pull him behind the curtains. While Wahib turns to us, he rubs his forehead and disturbs his comb-over, his hair flying everywhere to show the baldpate underneath. Tahir also rubs his face. The cockiness leaves him and he looks nervous.

"Listen, we're running a business," Wahib says when he steps back inside the main part of the store.

"And we're enforcing the law," I say.

"I promise you those are only dance videos," he says, his voice smooth and charming. What a fake.

"Why don't you play them?" Nasreen asks, jutting her chin towards a TV and VCR.

"No, no, that's unnecessary," Tahir says. "They're very long, and I'm sure neither of us has time to view them. Also, some of them involve belly dancing—this is a store specializing in Middle Eastern entertainment—and I wouldn't want to offend you ladies. We're just running an innocent business, I swear."

"Belly dancing my ass," Nasreen mutters under her breath.

"We've already seen your business side when you wanted to sell us that Umm Kulthum tape for a hundred bucks, and when we couldn't afford it you wanted a sleazy trade," I say. "You wanted me!"

"Okay, okay, I'm sorry about that," Wahib says. "You can't say that you're unattractive and that no man would take a chance like that. How about we strike a bargain? A real one."

"I don't know, sir," Nasreen says. "We take our jobs seriously."

"Yeah, we need to take you and your brother down to the station," I say. "We'll also call in our team to confiscate all your goods in the backroom."

"There's no need for that." Wahib flashes us a charming smile. "We both can get what we want today."

***

It's done all the time, or so I've heard. Businesses pay off mafia men or the police. We receive our own bribe, and we leave with the tape. It's in my purse, like a block of gold. I'm so happy I could cry. We're no fools, not anymore. We played it before we left, listening with headphones from Tahir's boom box. It's Umm Kulthum all right, the same songs that were on the destroyed tape and five extra songs we'll leave out when we make a copy. All it cost us were the subway tokens to get here, because the men gave it to us for nothing. Nasreen also demanded the tape of me on NYC Dance Off, which I'll ask her to put in a safe place until I leave. My first instinct was to destroy it in case someone found it, but I want memories of my first kiss with a possible boyfriend.

We stand at a corner two blocks from the store, waiting for Abe. A few minutes later, he walks out of the store with a paper bag.

"They still let you keep that?" I ask him when he joins us.

"Yes," he says. "They looked pissed but apologized for the misunderstanding I saw. They also gave me my money back to make up for the grief that was caused during that scene."

Nasreen and I look at each other. We hug. Then Abe

joins us for a group hug. We make a collective sigh of relief. Nasreen's hair is limp, as is mine. My limbs feel like spaghetti. Even Abe is sweating bullets after his feat. It's not every day that people pretend to be in a phony sting operation. We weren't there long, but I'm exhausted.

"I have to ask my uncle if I can go with you to the Madonna concert," I say. "That would be something. She's the reason I'm in this predicament in the first place. Well, I'm to blame, really."

"And I was your accomplice," Nasreen says. "I should've been more careful with my dad's tapes."

The sun peaks out of the clouds. It's still a grim, rainy day, with brief moments of sunshine. Abe rides with us on the first train. I hold his hand until he has to get off at his stop.

"Where do you want to go today?" Nasreen asks. "You want to see Greenwich Village? There's also time to see the Statue of Liberty."

"No," I say. "I don't want to go anywhere. I've had enough adventure today."

"Me too."

"There are two more things to do during the rest of my stay, and that's it for me," I say. "Go see Madonna and get you out of New York."

Chapter Twenty-Three

So much sneaking around. I'm tired of it.

Years ago when I was ten, my middle brother Naveen and I broke one of my dad's records. Actually, I can't blame him. It was all my fault. We had a pillow fight, which escalated into throwing objects. He threw a teddy bear at me, and in a moment of craziness I threw a record at him. It broke in half. My father walked in and yelled at us. It was a disco record, something he didn't care for. He told us to put the room straight, and that was it. I didn't end up all over town looking for a replacement for the record.

In a week I'll be back in Miami, where my suburban life is nowhere close to being as exciting as *Miami Vice*—that's one exciting show, putting Miami in everyone's minds, but unfortunately in the suburbs there's no Crockett and Tubbs and all the action they bring. In New York, life is as exciting as a TV show, but not in Miami. Life will be quiet. My parents will shelter me, as they've been doing all along. I'll be with my friends, who are goody-goodies like me, and my best friends who constantly put me down. I'll play soccer and win games, in the safe haven of my soccer team that's been stable with pretty much the same players year after year, with new people to replace the graduating seniors.

As crazy as my stay in New York has been, I know I'll miss it. The fast pace, from meeting Abe on the plane to the victory of getting the Kulthum replacement tape, has been nonstop.

Back in Nasreen's bedroom, she mentions a conversation she had with her parents.

"Hey, my mom and dad were talking about you last night," she says. "They were thinking of calling your parents to extend your stay since they like you being here, and they think it's good to have someone my age to hang with. Maybe you can change the date on your ticket and stay here for another week or two."

I shake my head. "No, I'm sorry, but I miss Miami."

"I thought you said it was boring and there wasn't much to do."

"It's still home." It's also a place where I don't get into so much trouble, but maybe after what I've been through I'll get into trouble more often. I love soccer, but it can't be the focus of my existence. I need to seek out more things—people and situations—in Miami, because surely I don't have to go across the country to live it up. I should be able to do that anywhere. Yes, I must step out of my comfort zone. I can't wake up, go to school, go to soccer practice, and be back home doing homework every single day with little or no variety to my schedule. Not only was getting the tape uplifting, but this thought also makes me smile: I can bring New York to Miami.

I'm touched that Uncle and Auntie want me to stay longer, but I'm determined to go home. I'm wrapping things up and winding down. Now I can breathe a little bit with this tape in my possession.

Uncle's at work and Nasreen is doing her audio magic in her closet. She copies songs from the tape onto a blank one, to match the arrangement of songs of the tape we destroyed. Following the songs on the original insert that we kept, Nasreen is recording everything in order. We don't want to hear Uncle say that anything is off, that he doesn't remember Song Y going before Song X.

The music coming from the closet is loud, and thankfully it doesn't bother anyone. It stopped raining, so Omar is outside playing with his friends. Auntie's taking a nap. She's a heavy sleeper and snores like a Mac truck. Good, because she won't interfere with us and walk in asking Nasreen to taste things for her. This makes me think that not only are we alone in our thoughts, but we're living separate lives in the city, inside homes, inside rooms of those homes. Yet sometimes everyone comes together. One way we converge is through music. I haven't met anyone who doesn't love it.

The music stops. My cousin bellows, "I'm finished!" Nasreen has the insert and she then digs around her closet for the case of the original... the original meaning Uncle's bootleg. There's all this music floating around all over the world in various media. An extraordinarily talented woman, who's no longer with us, sang. And the world heard her. Thousands of miles away from Egypt, in another country, two clueless teenage girls destroyed a piece of her. Of course, people can replicate those pieces ad infinitum. Yet from what I experienced trying to get her music, it seems like her songs are as precious as diamonds.

"Found it," Nasreen says, emerging from her closet. Her hair is flat on her head from scraping against heavy coats until she found the cassette case.

"You have the insert too?" I ask.

"Yup."

"Where's the dubbed tape?"

I take the new bootleg cassette from her hand and fit it into the case. Sure cassettes are supposed to fit into holders without a hitch, but this juncture seems magical. It feels like I've been solving the hardest jigsaw puzzle in the world and I put in the last piece. Last year I solved a Rubik's cube by breaking apart the pieces and putting them back together, which was cheating. This isn't. I worked hard for this moment.

Feeling emotional, tears well up in my eyes. Looking at Nasreen, her face becomes solemn as well.

"This is over," I say.

"This has certainly been an irregular summer," she says.

"We did it."

"Yes, we did." Nasreen breaks out into a grin.

I smile back, sniffling back the tears. We hug each other and then leave the room to put the tape in its rightful place, where Uncle can find it the next time he's in the mood for his favorite singer.

Chapter Twenty-Four

With the relief of getting the tape in order, Nasreen and I decide to go ahead with our college mission since it's still early in the day. Also, we're on fire after completing the major task of replacing the tape. "We need Omar," I say.

"Okay, let's get him," Nasreen says, a smirk on her face.

We do the unthinkable, something we wouldn't have done last week. We march over to the playground, through the open gate, and stop at a wall where Omar's playing handball. We're on his turf, which is okay since we have dirt on him. How many times has he snooped on Nasreen, opened her door to peek in on her, and tattled on her? We'll do the same to him.

He's in the middle of a lineup of boys. He doesn't see us or stop. Bounce. Bounce. Bounce. The balls waltz up and down.

Nasreen clears her throat, which doesn't do any good because as she does so an ice cream truck drives by, its tinkling music washing over the boys like magic. It isn't my or Nasreen's presence that makes the boys stop playing.

"Ice cream!" Omar yells in a war cry.

The boys charge towards the fence, completely ignoring us, and end up on the edge of the sidewalk where the truck has stopped. In minutes, all the boys have push pops and ice cream cones.

I can't wait anymore. "Omar!" I say, sprinting to where he is.

The boys look at us, their mouths crusted with orange, red, and blue ice cream. Nasreen fusses at her brother.

"We told you to be on call when we needed you..." she begins.

Omar looks comical with ice cream dribbling down his chin. He doesn't look like the mighty ringleader of his gambling troupe or a bossy younger brother, favorite of the family.

"Come on, Nasreen," he says. "You see that I'm in the middle of a game."

"In the middle of business," I say.

"Okay, I'll come with you," he concedes.

"Let's go," Nasreen commands. "We need to prepare. Dad will be home soon for dinner."

"I don't need time to prepare!" Omar says. "I know what we're going to do. I don't have to leave right now. I can stay out here a little longer."

"No, you can't!" Nasreen counters. She puts her brother into a headlock, his demon whorls facing me. I take my camera out of my purse and snap a picture. A fire hydrant is gushing in the background. A man walks by with a boom box on his shoulders. The clouds have cleared up, and it's summertime in all its sunny glory. Omar's friends laugh and point.

"Wuss," one of them calls out.

"Ha-ha, beaten up by a girl," another boy says. I count ten boys, all around the same age but varying in height and hair color. They seem to be enjoying their leader getting this dose of humiliation.

"What are you doing?" Nasreen asks, turning to me. "Did you take a picture of us?"

"No," I lie. Yes, I took a picture of this light moment— after days of living in fear and working hard to get the tape, this all seems fun in comparison. Nasreen is sour and wouldn't understand that I like her spunk, and even Omar's brattiness has a charm to it.

"Do you have the creature?" Nasreen asks.

"Yes," Omar says. He pulls out a medicine bottle with said creature in it.

Nasreen frowns, and I shiver with disgust. We need the moth for tonight, when we convince Auntie and Uncle that Nasreen is meant to go to an out-of-state college.

"Let's go," Nasreen says. She grabs Omar by the ear and pulls him as if he's on a leash. Omar doesn't resist but plays along. He's always seemed older than his age, but now he acts like a true eight-year-old whose sister is bossing him around. What's Omar going to do when he's younger and smaller than she is? He opens his mouth and proves he's mostly talk.

"You should be glad Asma is here," he says. "You just made me look bad in front of my friends."

"You can't always be the boss," Nasreen says.

"Yeah, Omar," I say. "You need to let people take turns being in charge." And it's clear we're in charge. For two weeks it's been the world against Nasreen and me, but now we're getting exactly what we want.

***

At home, Auntie seeks Nasreen. "How's the rice?" she asks.

Nasreen is being good. She's not making faces or being sarcastic as she tastes rice, gravy, and salad. While Nasreen is taste-testing, I'm in and out of the alcove. For the first time I walk freely into Omar's space, the curtains swishing back and forth as we get ready for tonight.

Uncle comes home and we eat dinner. Auntie has made a stir-fry of rice and vegetables. It's juicy and spicy. I'm truly enjoying food now that I don't have to think about Uncle not being able to find a tape after dinner, when he's in the mood to listen to music.

"Let me make the tea," Nasreen says when everyone's finished.

"Thank you!" Auntie says. Nasreen partakes in cleaning chores but rarely does anything in the kitchen. There's the clatter of a teakettle and cups as Nasreen gets everything ready. The steam makes the small apartment even warmer.

Everyone sits in the living room. Nasreen fixes a plate of pastries as the kettle toots. "Mom, why don't you read tea leaves for us?" Nasreen asks.

"I'd love to!" Auntie says.

I raise my eyebrows since Nasreen doesn't believe in those superstitions, but she pulls it off. She sounds interested enough, and her mom doesn't question her daughter's request. "I love having tea leaves read," I act along.

Nasreen is back in the living room, bringing in two cups of tea for her parents. After she serves them, she goes back to get tea for the rest of us.

Omar nibbles on baklava as he watches his parents finish off the tea while Dan Rather reports the news. The volume is low as Uncle loudly slurps his tea, while Auntie sips daintily. I blow on my cup, not interested in drinking. I want to see what's about to unfold, this thing Nasreen, Omar, and I are orchestrating. I perk up when Auntie is done with her cup of tea.

"Okay, here we have some leaves," she says.

"Read my fortune!" Nasreen demands, smiling as she sits on the arm of the chair I'm occupying.

"Okay..." Auntie hums and then frowns as she peers into the bottom of the cup. "This is strange."

"What is it?" Uncle asks.

"I could swear the tea leaves are not forming pictures, but words."

Uncle takes his last slurp and looks into his cup, which he rotates in his hands. Where I'm sitting, I can see the tea leaves making a moist mess at the bottom of their cups. "My cup looks like it says something too," he says.

"Free," Auntie says in Farsi.

"Nasreen," Uncle says.

"Free Nasreen," Auntie repeats.

"This is impossible," Uncle says, "but this is what it's saying."

"But free Nasreen how?" Auntie wonders.

"Do you think this means..." Uncle trails off.

The two are frowning, pondering two words that formed in their separate cups. We've made them think things over. Months of Nasreen wondering if she could leave and then me hearing about her problem for days might finally be over. I hope this is working.

Once we had something to blackmail Omar with, I incorporated him into my plan. My bratty little cousin had taken glue, wrote FREE at the bottom of one cup and NASREEN at the bottom of the other. Then he poured loose leaves onto the glue and shook out the excess. I remember doing that in art class anytime I decorated with glitter. The cups dried overnight, and we made sure Omar used Krazy Glue so the glue wouldn't melt off easily from the tea. And tonight Nasreen didn't use more loose tea like the kind Auntie or Uncle normally use but a tea bag so the tea leaves we adhered to the bottom wouldn't be obscured.

Nasreen's lips twitch as she suppresses a smile. I'm doing the same, forcing a straight face. "Wow," I say. "The tea leaves are trying to tell us something."

"Maybe Nasreen needs to go to the college she wants," Omar says.

Uncle shakes his cup, but those tea leaves are there to stay until someone pulls them off along with the glue. Auntie has many tea cups, so if the glue doesn't peel away—and it shouldn't since it's Krazy Glue—we'll dispose of them. They served their purpose tonight.

"Let me see what this says," Omar says, grabbing the

free cup from his mother's fingers. "I can't see too well." He walks over to the window and pulls the blinds up so that he can see better. On the right pane is a moth.

Auntie gasps. Even Uncle raises his eyebrows in shock.

My mother once told me that a moth on the right side means something good, while on the left side it's ominous. There was once a moth stuck on the right side of our patio all day long, so Mom told me something good was going to happen. If I got all As on a report card or if Dad got a promotion, then that was confirmed. To me she was just seeking things to solidify her suspicions, much like how Auntie does. This superstition is working well for Nasreen's case. Also, it's a good thing the moth is on the outside, where Omar had tacked the dead thing onto the window with adhesive. Yes, he had murdered a moth for us. I shiver with insect heebie-jeebies.

"These are signs," Auntie says.

"I don't know about that," Uncle says. "But maybe we should rethink allowing Nasreen to go to another state."

"Why not? She's smart and responsible."

"We have family in California who can help her."

"My sister lives in Boston."

"We have relatives in at least five states to look out for her."

We don't want to press things. We let Uncle and Auntie stew in their conversation now the signs have convinced them to be more open on the issue of Nasreen's college choices.

While Auntie and Uncle continue to discuss Nasreen's good qualities and where she could possibly go, we clear the table, squirreling away the cups so there's no investigation and no one discovers the glue.

"The sun is hurting my eyes," Omar says, pulling the blinds down.

"I'll take out the garbage," Nasreen says. She'll also swipe the moth off the window to make it look like it flew away. Everything's going as planned.

"Yes, we'll talk further about this tomorrow," Uncle says.

"We'll look at exactly where Nasreen wants to go if she has her heart set on leaving us," Auntie says. "My baby leaving us."

"Our firstborn..." Uncle sighs.

Auntie wails, both happy and sad that Nasreen may finally get what she wants by leaving the basement apartment. Nasreen isn't even done with high school yet, with one more year to go, and they sound like she's ready to depart. She actually is ready, since it's all she's been thinking about, but it won't be until next summer that she'll go away. It's a major milestone that her parents have shifted on the idea of her leaving. I didn't think it would happen. She was born a few blocks away at St. Luke's, we've walked by her elementary school multiple times during our treks around the city... I might be ecstatic to be here, but I can imagine that if a place is too familiar a person will eventually want to leave it.

"Thank you," Nasreen mouths silently when she comes back. I'm thrilled that my idea worked. We'll soon see if our other endeavor panned out or not. Uncle gets up to look through his cassette collection.

"I want to listen to some music," he says. "What happened tonight is too heavy for me to continue thinking about."

"It's a time to celebrate though," Auntie says. "This reminds me of myself at Nasreen's age. I also went off to college."

"That was a different time," Uncle says.

"Uncle, the world will always be dangerous," I say. "You must admit that even in your country bad things happened. It might be a different atmosphere here, but people can take precautions, and they'll be fine. You raised Nasreen well. She's careful around people, and she's always aware of her surroundings. Whenever I'm out with her I feel safe."

Nasreen gives me another grateful look, her top lip sucked in and her eyes teary. I meant what I said. Nasreen has a tough exterior—too tough at times, because I think she's excessively guarded and occasionally rude—and I can't imagine any person or situation knocking her down.

"Time for music!" Uncle says. "How about some Umm Kulthum? I haven't heard her in a while."

"Oh yes," Auntie gushes.

"Omar! Nasreen! Help me get everything off these shelves so I can find my Umm Kulthum tape behind the entertainment center."

"What are you talking about?" Nasreen asks. "It's not there."

"Yes, it is," Uncle says. "Remember I checked not too long ago. It's not in those boxes."

"You need to look harder," I say. "Maybe it's on the bottom."

"I'm sure you overlooked it," Nasreen says.

"Let me help you look," I say. I dip my hand inside a box, pretend I'm digging around when I know exactly where it is, and pull it out. This cassette, that I ran all over town for, that I was harassed by those two brothers for, that almost cost me a lot of money, that made me go to that dreadful audition, that put me on TV for the country to see me kissing a boy... such a small thing put me through all this.

"Play it," Nasreen urges.

"That's not my Umm Kulthum tape," Uncle says. "To clarify... it is, but it isn't."

Nasreen's face falls and my heart sinks. I feel sick. How can he tell when he hasn't played it yet? We must have done something wrong. I study the outside of the cassette to see if we missed anything, but in all appearances this is the tape. It's the same case, same insert, and the replacement is the same color and brand as the original. But Uncle knows. We aren't able to trick him. We've been caught.

Chapter Twenty-Five

"That's not the tape," Uncle says, shaking his head. He wipes his hand across his tired face. His lids and mouth are drooping.

"Dad, I'm sorry," Nasreen says.

"Yeah, me too," I say.

"For what?" he asks. "That's not the tape."

A hush falls through the apartment. Even Omar is attentive, his hand on his curtains as he's about to leave us to play his games. Auntie blinks in her silence. The tremendous thing that Nasreen and I did—but mainly me—cannot be shirked so easily. Sure I thought I could easily cover up this deed, thinking a tape's a tape, that we just have to match it song for song, but it's not that easy. Uncle's tape is probably years old and carries memories. The songs may be the same, but a replacement is a clone without personality.

"It's my fault the tape's missing," Uncle says. "Now, please, help me take everything off the shelf."

"Why?" I say. "The original tape isn't going to appear. This is the tape. Well, not really. Let me explain the damage..."

"I know about the damage," Uncle says.

"You do?" Nasreen says. "Of course you do. She's your favorite singer."

"Which is why I replaced the tape years ago," he says.

"Huh?"

"What?"

Nasreen and I look at each other. What is Uncle talking about?

"That tape you're holding was damaged by my sister years ago," Uncle says. "She took it to a wedding where she sang. She erased parts of the beginning on side 1 and the middle of side 2 with her horrible singing. I can't even bear to listen to it. I tried to let it go, but I'm still resentful. How could she not read the label and realize that my favorite songs were on it?"

"Yeah, how silly," Nasreen says.

As everything dawns on me, I feel pretty stupid, yet also relieved.

"I got that cassette shortly after coming to this country, and I don't want to throw it out. I don't listen to it anymore because of the damage, but I leave it in my collection. Anyway, help me find my other Kulthum tape."

With three pairs of hands we quickly pile records, cassettes, books, and videos to the side. Lastly, Uncle unplugs the TV and pulls it out. Nasreen and Uncle grab each side of the entertainment center and pull it away from the wall. I reach in, since the shelves have no backing, and pull out several tapes that had fallen to the floor. Dust bunnies cover them. I shriek when a spider scuttles away.

On the tapes there are pictures of a guy with a full beard, a young guy holding a banjo, and then I see her. This doesn't look like a bootleg. The cassette has a picture of Umm Kulthum on the cover, and she looks beautiful in an evening gown, with her head poised upwards as if she's a queen. Her hair's in a bun and her profile is regal.

"That's my other Umm Kulthum tape," Uncle says, taking it from me. "This is the one I bought after my sister ruined the other."

All that worrying and running around for nothing, for a tape that Uncle's sister had destroyed. I'm ambivalent with feelings of relief, regret, and idiocy. I squash those feelings down. I wouldn't have auditioned for that show, and it was fun practicing my dance moves. Those porn brothers were icky and scary, but my time with them toughened me up, and I'm grateful to have had a *Cagney & Lacey* moment. I wouldn't have met Abe again. He wouldn't have offered us Madonna tickets.

When the entertainment system is back in place, I put the boxes of cassettes on shelves and stack the records into neat piles. Uncle bends down and puts the newer, undamaged, authentic Umm Kulthum tape into his stereo. When he presses Play I hear her gorgeous voice. It's crystal clear, unlike the tape we destroyed. Uncle's sister, an aunt who lives in Toronto who I've only seen on two occasions, didn't really sound bad on the tape we destroyed, but the difference is there. Umm Kulthum makes me teary-eyed. Even though I only know a few words, I know she's singing about the heart, about being human, with every emotion compounded into her voice the same way a prism catches and releases light.

"What a voice," Nasreen says.

Uncle puts our replacement tape back in the box, where he'll never pick it up since he thinks his sister's voice is on it. Maybe when he wears out his Kulthum tape, we'll tell him the truth and he can use our tape for real.

Auntie washes dishes, and Omar retires to his alcove now that this tape issue is over, or "ov-a" as many would say in New York. Uncle, Nasreen, and I sit on the sofa listening. Since Uncle's in a good mood after finding his tape, we spring our Madonna request on him.

"You know that Asma loves Madonna?" Nasreen says. "She loves Madonna the way you love Umm."

"It's true, Uncle," I say.

"Who's Madonna?" Uncle asks.

He reads the national and international portions of the

newspaper, and the only TV he watches is the news, alongside his Middle Eastern entertainment videos. During my last visit he let me know that he wasn't aware of who Michael Jackson was.

"I forgot to bring her tape, or I'd let you listen," I say.

"She's playing in Madison Square Garden in a few days," Nasreen says. "It would be a shame if Asma couldn't see her."

"I agree." Uncle nods. "If Umm Kulthum were alive today, I would do anything to see her in concert again."

"So, anyway, while we were out we came across this guy who offered us tickets," I say. "He's from Miami too."

"Do you know him? Who is this guy?" He raises his voice in alarm. What were the two of us doing talking to boys? How about they're half the population?

"Dad, don't worry. We bumped into the guy. He's Syrian and our age, by the way, and he has some extra tickets. He's staying with his aunt and uncle the same way Asma is."

We had to throw in the Syrian bit since that would sway Uncle more, since he's partial to having Middle Eastern friends. "I'd have to meet this boy," he says. "I don't like the idea of my daughter and niece out with some stranger, some boy."

"A nice boy with tickets, Dad."

"Yeah, Uncle, he was real polite when we waited in line somewhere in midtown. You'll like him. And please, Uncle, let us go. Madonna's my favorite singer."

"Okay. I'm not really comfortable with this idea, but let me see this boy and I'll think about it after I talk to him."

***

Later that night, in the closet while we're watching Letterman and eating lokum, Nasreen and I go over our day.

"I feel super-duper dumb over what happened with the tape," Nasreen says, prying her teeth apart. My mouth is also gummy from lokum. "I had no idea my aunt destroyed that tape and that Dad no longer listens to it. I wasn't aware he replaced the tape. It was literally under our noses this whole time."

"How were we supposed to know it was a poor quality tape when it was a bootleg?" I ask. "We couldn't know. And when you're listening to someone foreign, you can't always tell who's singing. I didn't know that was my other aunt singing in the beginning of the cassette."

"That tape put us through a lot, but at least it's all over," Nasreen says. "We need to call Abe so he can meet my father. It sounds like he'll let us go to this concert."

"It does."

We lick the powder off our fingers. My tongue travels across my teeth, picking pistachio pieces out of my mouth. Even though we've been staying up until three or four o'clock, we'll go to bed earlier tonight. We're both exhausted after we took care of the tape, changed the minds of Nasreen's parents, and requested Uncle's permission to see Madonna. I wrote half of a letter to my mom, which I'll finish tomorrow. All I'm writing is that I'm doing well and Nasreen is a great tour guide. I'll mail it in the morning. It'll be my last letter to her since in a week I'll be back in Miami. I haven't bothered to write Tamara and Misty any other letters since I haven't received any from them. With the remaining quarters I have I might call them again before I leave, and that's it. Even though my stay in New York and their treatment of me has made me question their friendship, I do plan to catch up with them when I get back home.

My relationships with my best friends may be shaky, but at least I'll have Abe in Miami. I'm totally going to stay in touch with him. This doesn't have to be a simple summer fling. It can be much more.

Chapter Twenty-Six

Uncle and Auntie decide it'll be okay if Nasreen goes to college in California, Texas, or Massachusetts, as long as she's not too far away from relatives who she can turn to in times of need. Now they're debating about apartment rentals or dorm rooms. Auntie believes in dorms, while Uncle thinks they're cesspools of alcohol and drug abuse. He'd like Nasreen to rent an apartment with a Muslim roommate. Everything is so far away, but they're planning, still trying to direct Nasreen's life.

"Let them act like they're in charge," Nasreen says. "Once I'm on my own and out of New York, that'll be my bliss. I'll get to do my own thing."

I like her philosophy. "I'm happy you got your way," I say.

"I couldn't have done it without you."

"I owed it to you, especially since everything was my fault. I whined about not having Madonna and you tried to help me out with that."

"That was an ordeal."

"It was," I agree.

We're in her room, and I stand by her desk as she organizes her college brochures and pamphlets. Now that her parents don't mind her leaving, she's pulling out the colleges that are in states that have relatives in them. "Can I have one of those brochures?" I ask.

"For that scrapbook of yours?" she asks.

"How do you know about my scrapbook?" I ask, alarmed that she knows about it when I thought I had been hiding it well underneath my pillows.

Nasreen shakes her head. "One night I woke up and heard you gluing, stapling, and taping. It's kind of funny. I don't know anyone else who does that, but who am I to judge? I watch TV in a closet at night. Don't worry, I haven't looked in it."

"It's not a diary," I say.

"But you treat it as one," she says.

"Yes, it's in pictorial code."

"Here, take this." She gives me a pamphlet for a school in Arizona. Since she knows about my scrapbook, I go ahead and work on it in front of her. I climb onto the top bunk and staple one side of the pamphlet onto a fresh page in a way that enables me to fold it out completely. I'll remember Nasreen and how I helped her with this goal. I have mementoes from my other stays in New York, but nothing like this. I usually collect maps of museums, tickets to plays, and other touristy things. What I've collected so far doesn't reflect me being a tourist. It's about me being an adventurer.

If Uncle allows me to go see Madonna, I'll tape or staple my ticket stub to the adjacent page. It will be the first concert I've ever gone to, and I'd be seeing my idol, so this will be a momentous event. I'm not sure what else I'll be doing in New York in my final days. Maybe I can really see museums and other sights—not lying to Uncle, Auntie, or Mom about it, but really going to these places now that I don't have to see the porn brothers again. Nasreen has already put back Auntie's grocery money we borrowed but never used, and since I didn't spend money on the porn brothers' tape, I have some cash for myself. The rest of my stay in Manhattan will be actual vacation time, in which I'm a tourist. I'll have no mission this time other than to enjoy the city.

"Asma!" Auntie yells from the living room.

I jump when I hear her voice. What if she wants me to taste something, even though Nasreen is the one she comes to for that? "Asma!" She bursts through the door, and I instinctively hold my scrapbook to my chest.

"You have mail," she tells me, reaching up to hand me a letter. It's Tamara's address and bubbly writing on the front. Finally, a letter from one of my friends.

Sitting on top of the bunk bed, I rip the letter open. It's actually two letters inside the envelope, one from Tamara and one from Misty. Tamara writes about how she's spent time at the recreation center by her house, playing sports and meeting guys. The whole letter is about herself.

Misty's letter is similar, about her exploits at the beach and kissing boys, but her writing is more abrasive, with her rough personality and putdowns shining through.

Asma, I wish you could be here. John's friend Billy isn't all that cute. He flirts with me, but I'm not into him and thought maybe you'd like him. There's also a soccer camp going on at our school, and I thought about you, since you only live and breathe soccer.

I'm fuming. Why would I want a boy who isn't good enough for her... he'd fit my lower standards instead? And I don't live and breathe soccer. I haven't even touched a soccer ball during my stay in New York. I turn five pages back in my scrapbook and find a picture of them. I'm standing in the middle of them, and they both have their fingers formed into Vs, making rabbit ears behind my head. I take a red pen and slash into the picture so hard I make rips. I draw devil horns and moustaches on my two friends. It's not enough, though. I need to have the courage to confront Misty and Tamara about their treatment of me. That's it; I've had it with both of them. I leap off the bed and find the remaining quarters from the pencil case.

"What are you doing?" Nasreen asks.

"I'm going to step out and make a call," I say.

Outside, I wait for a man to get off the phone and then

dial Misty's number. I have issues with both my friends, but Misty is the bigger problem with her attitude and rudeness.

"Hey, Asma!" Misty says. She sounds excited to hear from me, but I don't feel it. She's not exuberant about our friendship. She probably gets her jollies from seeing me as a doormat and punching bag.

"Hey, is it her?" Tamara asks. "Move over so we can share the receiver... I'm staying with Misty for the day. I'm glad you called when we're both here."

"What are you up to?" Misty asks.

"I'm getting ready to see Madonna," I say. "Someone offered me and my cousin tickets."

"No way," Tamara says.

"Madonna's overrated," Misty says. "And she's a slut."

"Yeah, she can be slutty," Tamara agrees.

They're criticizing my idol? Madonna has more talent, intelligence, and personality in her pinky finger than the two of them combined. "I can't wait to go," I say. "Oh, and I'm going with a guy."

"You?" Tamara says. Misty snorts in disbelief.

"I've actually been doing a lot in New York, things you wouldn't believe, but you never let me get in a word, and it took forever for the two of you to write back to me."

"Hey, don't be sore," Tamara says. "We can't help it if you call from some shitty payphone."

"What are you talking about?" Misty asks. "Of course we listen to you, but it's not like you have anything great to share with us. If you want to tell us what you've been doing, then just say it already."

Please deposit twenty-five cents.

I jab a quarter into the coin slot. "You know what, screw the both of you!" I say. "I don't want to be interrupted, and I don't want my so-called friends to disbelieve my adventures. And yeah, I had adventures. And you know what, I think I was able to have them because I wasn't anywhere near the two of you!"

I slam the receiver down to hang up on them. I wasn't even really thinking when I got that off my chest, but standing here and reflecting on my outburst, I realize I'm right. It was my traveling here alone and then being in the supportive, loving, fun-filled care of my cousin that allowed me to break loose and live a little. If Tamara and Misty had accompanied me on this trip, I'd be on the backburner, watching the two of them kiss boys and get into trouble. I'd be the goody-goody in the corner not saying or doing much.

Sayonara, Tamara and Misty. There's no way I'll continue being friends with them. I deserve better. There are other girls at school I've been meaning to sit with during lunch. The girls on my soccer team have been asking me to meet with them at the mall or at parties, but I would say no because I was always following Tamara and Misty, wasting my time on those two when they never thought much about me. Well, I'm through with them. New York has given me so much, tested me, taught me, and now I also have this gift. I kicked two rotten people out of my life.

***

Abe isn't able to meet my family right away since he has his own familial obligations, but he comes to the basement a few hours before the concert starts to see if Uncle will approve of him. I can't think there's anything to disapprove of, unless Uncle has something against cuteness and rattails.

Auntie smiles and serves him tea while Uncle grills him on where he's from, what his grades are, and what he wants to be when he's grown up. He's taking us to a concert. I'm not marrying the guy! Uncle's eyes light up when Abe tells him he wants to be a doctor.

"It's always good to have doctors in the family," Uncle says.

"Yeah," Nasreen says. "If you need a spleen to be taken out or a leg amputated, family can do it for you."

Why does she have to act weird in front of my more-than-a-summer-fling? "Can we go, Uncle?" I say.

"I think it would be all right if you took my daughter and niece to this concert," Uncle finally approves. Nasreen and I don't waste time. While he continues to talk to Abe, we go to her room to dress.

Nasreen wears all black while I'm in hot pink from head to toe, with tights and a ballerina skirt. Abe looks absolutely hot with a white tank top and black jeans. I playfully pull on his rattail during the subway ride. I'm nervous. I'm about to see Madonna in concert. I've idolized this woman from afar. Just like Helen of Troy launched a thousand ships, Madonna is technically the person who launched my crazy summer vacation.

First, we have dinner, and then we head to the concert location. Seeing Madonna live is a crazy experience. It's a million times better than seeing her on TV or listening to her on the radio. From a lost tape to seeing her live! She looks gorgeous from what I can see in our nosebleed seats, and she sounds amazing. She's not one of those singers who sounds horrible live, and she doesn't need to lip-sync and fake anything. Even as she bounces across the stage, she doesn't seem out of breath and her voice doesn't break. She's pure, real talent.

Abe grabs my hand. I don't know how Nasreen will react to me kissing him since she can be rude and aggressive. Also, she didn't seem happy when our kiss was caught on tape. She's busy looking at the stage and her surroundings, but I don't want to be intimate in front of her. The lights turn real dim, and that's when I dare to kiss Abe in public... again.

"Who's That Girl?" Madonna asks.

I'm that girl, I answer in my head. I'm the one who's where I want to be and who I want to be with.

Made in the USA
Lexington, KY
16 August 2017